Praise for

The Loblolly Boy

'The children in *The Loblolly Boy* find themselves
caught up in a remarkable chain of events. Through
an encounter with the fantastic loblolly boy they can
become fantastic themselves. This is a rich fantasy –
alive with original twists, surprises and mysteries
which I dare not reveal. Children's literature is
about to be enriched with a new classic.'
Margaret Mahy

'I loved it! It was fun, exciting, thrilling and
strangely realistic – as though there really was
such a thing as a loblolly boy.'
Edward, 11

'A unique story that is a real page-turner . . . I loved
the happy ending . . . an awesome storyline.'
Georgia, 12

THE LOBLOLLY BOY

James Norcliffe

ALLEN&UNWIN

This edition published in 2009

First published in New Zealand by Longacre Press, 2009

Allen & Unwin
83 Alexander Street
Crows Nest NWS 2065
Australia
Phone: (61 2) 8425 0100
Fax: (61 2) 9906 2218
Email: info@allenandunwin.com
Web: www.allenandunwin.com

National Library of Australia Cataloguing-in-Publication entry:
Norcliffe, James, 1946-
The loblolly boy / James Norcliffe.
ISBN 978 1 74237 116 0 (pbk.)
For children.
NZ 823.2

Cover and text design by Bruno Herfst
Cover photograph: Getty Images/Clay Patrick McBride
Set in 11.2/15 pt Adobe Garamond by Midland Typesetters, Australia
Printed in Australia by McPherson's Printing Group

2 4 6 8 10 9 7 5 3

For Keiller and Meredith –
the Flying Burrito Sisters

PROLOGUE

THE HOUSE was now completely empty. The furniture removal men had carried everything outside and loaded it into the huge truck parked in the drive. Packers had been in to his room and packed his entire life into large cardboard cartons. His clothes, his books, his board games. The football boots, tennis racquets and hockey sticks were all stowed away. The men had packed his pictures. One woman had pulled his posters off the wall leaving little blue stains where the Blu Tack had been. His posters of steam locomotives were gone. There was no longer a black-and-white poster of Charlie Chaplin sitting miserably on a broken-down stoop with a white dog beside him. The picture was from a film called *A Dog's Life*. He'd never seen it, but he didn't have to: he knew about dogs' lives. It was what he'd been leading ever since the woman, Janice, came into his father's life.

Then the removal men had taken away the furniture. His bed. His dresser. The empty bookshelves.

Without all of his stuff, his room felt very strange. Bigger in some ways, smaller in others. There was also an unpleasant echoing emptiness that made him want to whisper.

He went and stood at the window, which looked out on to the backyard. There hadn't been much to strip there, so it still looked as if the Great Change hadn't yet taken place. But as soon as he turned back and saw the desolation of his empty room he could not deny it.

He put the box down on the carpet and knelt beside it. The one thing he had point-blank refused to let the removal men take away was his Hornby train set. Now, he took the lid off the box and admired the set once more. The cache of rails that clipped together to make a large oval track. The flat-deck wagon, the passenger carriage, the oil tanker and, best of all, the beautiful engine with the little coal-bunker that went with it. The engine was racing-green, with gunmetal-black and shining brass trims. It was perfect. It was his most treasured possession. The train had originally belonged to his father and as a very small child the boy had never been allowed to play with it. But when his father, a couple of years previously, had brought the box to his room and laid it carefully on his bed, the boy knew that he had become grown-up enough to be trusted with it. And it was a trust he had never abused. How could he? The train set was such a precious thing.

Without really thinking about what he was doing, the boy took out some sections of the rails and the little push clips that fastened them together. Almost automatically, he began to assemble the track. Some part of him, the reckless part, knew that this was something he must do. One last time. It was as though he were taking part in a necessary ceremony. Another part of him, the nervous part, knew he was being crazy. There was no time. The big truck had already left and the house had been cleaned. They were supposed to leave so the new owners could shift in. That afternoon they were going to a motel before driving all the next day and the next to their new home several hundred kilometres north.

Before very long the track was completely assembled. Doggedly, he wound up the engine's clockwork mechanism, then he placed the little locomotive gently on the track. He coupled the coal wagon to it, then coupled the other wagons to the coal wagon. At last all was done. Carefully he moved the brake lever and the locomotive began its clickety-clackety circuit around the track. The boy sat back and sighed, following the almost hypnotic passage of the train as it sped round and round like the remorseless second hand on a large, forbidding clock.

All at once, the bedroom door swung open and his father stood there. When he saw the boy sitting on the floor of the bare room with the Hornby train set assembled and working, his jaw dropped in astonishment.

'Ben!' he cried. 'What on earth do you think you're doing?'

The boy looked up and was about to try to explain when he saw the woman, Janice, attracted by his father's tone, appear at his father's shoulder. Immediately the boy turned away and gave his full attention to the train.

The voice of the woman echoed about the empty room. 'Is the boy stark raving mad?' she exclaimed. 'Doesn't he realise we should have been out of here an hour ago? Hasn't he noticed that I've been working my fingers to the bone trying to get this bloody place presentable for the new people – who'll be here at any minute, I might add!'

'Janice,' said his father. 'It's okay.'

'If you think it's okay,' she snapped, 'you're as loopy as he is!' Then, abruptly, she turned and left.

'Ben,' said his father. 'Not a good idea, mate. Let's get this thing packed up as quickly as possible, hey? Stop the train now. Let's get it all back in the box . . .'

The boy didn't trust himself to speak. All the same he picked up the train and pulled the brake lever to one side so that the wheels stopped whirring around. He placed the little locomotive gently in the section of the box shaped for it, then did the same for the other rolling stock. His father, meanwhile, quickly and efficiently dismantled the track and stowed the rails and clips away. Then he put the cover back on the box.

'I can't understand how this wasn't packed up and put in the removal van,' he said. 'God knows what we'll do with it.'

Then he saw the expression on his son's face. And realised. 'Whoops, Ben,' he said. 'Not a smart move. Not a smart move at all. We'll be really lucky to fit this in the car, you know. Janice has hardly a spare inch left with all the stuff we're going to need on the trip.'

The boy looked at his father with alarm, then a sickening feeling took over as he realised what his father was suggesting.

'You're joking. You're joking aren't you, Dad?'

His father looked sad and lost, and the boy understood that he wasn't joking at all.

'Dad?'

The motel was on a busy road on the outskirts of the city. It seemed to be in the middle of an entire country called

Motel. From his upstairs bedroom the boy could look up and down the street: flashing neon as far as he could see was advertising *Vacancy* or *No Vacancy* and *Spa Pool* and *Sky TV*. It disappointed him that none of the signs was advertising *Janice Removal* or *New Life*. He had no idea what time it was, but it was late. His father and Janice were downstairs in the little motel living room with the television turned up loudly.

Earlier his father had come up to the bedroom and handed him a package. It was the Hornby engine wrapped in a tea towel.

'I've persuaded Janice to let you keep the engine,' he'd said. 'It won't take up that much room.'

The boy had stared at his father in disbelief. His father's voice had had the expression of someone who had won a major victory. Did he realise what he was actually saying? Victory or not, his father couldn't meet his son's eyes. 'We'll look around when we get up north,' he'd added. 'Might be able to pick up some things there . . .'

His father hadn't waited to explain. He'd whispered, 'Goodnight, then . . .' and hurriedly left.

The boy had refused to cry. Instead, he'd summoned up a bitter hatred. He hadn't bothered to unwrap the engine. He didn't even want to look at it. He'd taken it wordlessly from his father and stowed it under his jersey. He knew he was being punished for holding Janice up. He knew the punishment was mean and vindictive, and way out of line for whatever nuisance he'd been; and he knew that his father had been powerless to do anything about it. He hated her. He hated his father, too, for being on her side.

He opened the door to the narrow balcony with the

wrought-iron railing that ran along in front of the upper storey of the motel. He went outside and breathed in the night air. The faint noise of the television reminded him that Janice was just a floor away. He walked along the balcony in front of one, two, three motel rooms and then down the steps to the drive. There was no sound of television here, just the swish, swish of tyres and the rumble of engines as traffic moved up and down the road. The drive was lined on one side with tall narrow yew trees. He was just about at the driveway entrance when he thought he saw a movement behind one of the trees.

He stopped, thinking it might have been a cat. Then he saw the shape again, and it was much bigger than a cat. It was a person, a little person.

'Who are you?' he asked nervously. 'What are you doing in there?'

A figure stepped into view. It was a boy about his own age. He looked as if he'd been to a fancy-dress party. He was wearing a long, flowing cape-like garment and he seemed to be wearing baggy leggings rather than pants or jeans.

'Been pretty tough, eh?' said the boy.

'What do you mean?'

'With that woman.'

'What woman?'

'I dunno. The woman in the motel with you. She looks really mean.'

'She *is* really mean,' said Ben.

'You know,' said the figure in the cape. 'I could get you away from her forever, if you really wanted to.'

Ben stared at him. Was he crazy? What did he mean?

'How?' he asked.

'Easy,' said the figure airily. 'Of course, you've got to really want to be rid of her . . .'

'I do,' said Ben bitterly, feeling the weight of the engine under his jersey. 'I really do.'

'Good,' said the figure.

Suddenly Ben felt a surge of alarm. It had been something the figure had said. What was it? He'd said 'rid of her'. 'Wait,' he said. 'It's not criminal, is it? I mean, you're not talking about anything violent . . .'

Realising what Ben was thinking, the other laughed. 'Oh, no,' he said. 'Not at all. We won't harm a hair on her head. It's just that you will never need to see her head again!' And then he laughed once more.

Ben stared at the boy. Although the drive was floodlit, there were still dark shadows beneath the yew trees, and the boy, perhaps deliberately, had not attempted to step into the light.

'Who are you?' Ben whispered, remembering he'd already asked that question and not received an answer.

The other stared at him. 'I'm the loblolly boy,' he said.

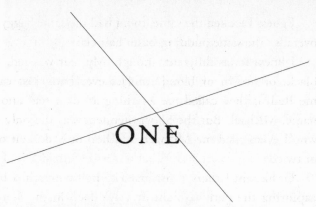

ONE

THE GARDEN was wild and large. There were tall, spreading trees, little lakes with water lilies, and rocky pathways. It would have been a paradise had it not been for the enormous wall that completely surrounded it. I don't know exactly how many of us lived in the Great House; perhaps a hundred. Kids came and went. It seemed, though, that I'd been there forever, at least as long as anybody else. Who were we? We were the unwanted, the not-wanted-on-voyage. The Great House was a place for abandoned kids to be dumped. Some kids were orphans; others were rejects. I'm not sure what I was. Probably a reject.

Most of the others avoided going deep into the Garden. Perhaps it was because they knew that sooner or later they would hit the wall, and didn't want to be reminded of it. Perhaps it was because the Keepers kind of frowned on people going too far from the Great House. But most likely it was because the others all liked to stick together, playing in a tight little clump, and not one of them would venture far from anybody else. So they stayed where they were, on the asphalt playground, all looking the same in their baggy red overalls.

I guess I looked the same, too. I had the same baggy red overalls. The same pudding-basin hair cut.

I knew I was different, though. My hair was red. Not black, or brown or blond. In fact everybody just called me Red, if they called me anything at all. I had another name: Michael. But the Superintendent was the only one who'd ever called me Michael, and he'd only done it once or twice.

Unlike the others, I preferred to be by myself. I liked exploring the pathways and byways deep in the Garden. Quite often, I even made it all the way to the wall. This far from the Great House the playful shouting and yelling of the other kids was just a faint buzzing, like the sound of insects, almost as if they were distant in time as well as space.

In a strange way I even liked the massive wall itself. It didn't frighten me, as it did so many of the others. Somehow it spoke to me of the world outside: told me it was there, was possible, even if I might never see it.

Sometimes, I would come across a Keeper or two. They would always look at me sourly, and demand to know why I wasn't with the others. I never had an answer that could satisfy them. Then they would wave an irritable hand at me as if I were some sort of low-life pest and tell me to get back to the Great House. Immediately.

Not once in my explorations of the Garden did I ever come across anybody but a Keeper.

Until the afternoon I found the loblolly boy.

He was sitting, back against the blotched trunk of an ancient tree that grew by a small lake. I could see straight away that he was just a boy, but in a weird way he looked almost as ancient as the tree. He appeared to be sleeping, but as I stopped in astonishment he turned and looked at me. It was his eyes. They were large and green and seemed filled with all the sadness of the world.

'Hello,' he said.

I was too startled by his presence in the Garden to return his greeting.

'How did you get here?' was all I could manage to whisper.

The figure lolling before me was dressed entirely in green: leaf-green leggings, a loose sage-green shirt, and a darker green cape of some filmy material. He didn't look at all angry.

'I flew across the wall,' he said.

That's, I guess, when I first thought that the loblolly boy was a little odd. Even stupid. I glanced across the little lake to where the great wall towered above the trees.

'I don't like people being sarcastic,' I said.

He nodded, his large green eyes studying me carefully.

'Of course not,' he said.

'Who are you?' I asked.

He shrugged. 'Does it matter?'

'It might,' I said. 'If they catch you.'

'If who catches me?'

I looked at him again with some surprise.

'The Keepers.' How could he not know about the Keepers? He could only have got there by sneaking past them somehow.

'They won't catch me.'

He said this with such certainty, he almost convinced me. I looked around as if expecting to see the black figures, the barking dogs, already moving determinedly towards us.

'Why not?'

'I'll fly away.'

It was the second time he'd mentioned flying. Stupid. He was so stupid. 'How did you really get here?' I asked again.

He looked at me thoughtfully. 'I've already told you,' he said.

I stared at him, trying to puzzle him out. There was something very unusual in the atmosphere, as though my ears were ringing, but all was still. The boy stood up, and then walked towards me. He was no taller than I was. If anything, he was a little smaller, and he was certainly slighter.

'What is your name?' I asked.

At first I thought he was going to fob me off again, but then he said, 'I'm the loblolly boy.'

'The what?'

'The loblolly boy. I'll teach you if you like.'

'Teach me what?'

'How to fly,' he said.

I gave a little grin. Back on to flying again. The loblolly boy stared at me gravely, then he smiled.

'Okay,' I said.

Why not humour him, I thought. It could be fun. It would be fantastic to have somebody new to play with. And pretending to fly would be a much better way of spending my time than the endless games of Four Square the others played on the asphalt courtyard in front of the big doors.

'When?' I said.

He shrugged. 'Tomorrow?'

'Where?'

'Here. If you can find this place again?'

I nodded. 'I reckon I can. You be careful though,' I added. 'If the Keepers find you here in the Garden there'll be a real big stink!'

He didn't understand.

'Big trouble,' I explained, and I drew my forefinger under my chin as if I were slitting my throat.

The loblolly boy understood, grinned and nodded. 'They'll never catch me,' he said once more. He seemed to believe it. Stupid.

><

So it was that the next day I made my way to the ancient tree by the little lake. I was a little surprised to find the loblolly boy there in exactly the same place. To tell the truth, the whole thing was so bizarre I almost convinced myself I'd daydreamed it.

'Hi,' I said.

'Hello. Are you ready?'

'Why not?'

I didn't know what I was expecting.

'You have to really want to fly. You know that, don't you?'

I grinned. This was off the wall . . . But as that thought crossed my mind, I saw behind him, across the little lake, the real wall: the towering stone barrier that had surrounded my life for as long as I could remember. And at that moment, I did want to fly. So, to humour him, I nodded. 'I really want to fly. I really do.' To fly up, up, and over . . .

The big green eyes studied me gravely.

'Are you sure?'

The question seemed to be both a challenge and a warning. The eyes continued to bore into me. This was getting just a little heavy. 'Of course!' I said hurriedly.

'Then stretch your arms out.'

I stretched my arms out like an aeroplane.

'Close your eyes.'

I closed my eyes.

'Jump!'

I jumped. I jumped half a metre, probably. Then I dropped down again. It was pathetic.

'Do it again!'

I tried once more with exactly the same result. Then I did it a third time. I opened my eyes to see if he was grinning. I was feeling stupid. Really stupid. Oddly enough, he was not grinning. He was staring at me with that same intense seriousness.

'Again!'

I was sick of it. 'No, this is silly.'

'You don't really want to fly.'

'It's just a game. We'd be better climbing trees and swinging from branch to branch. That'd be more like flying.'

'You don't know what flying is like.'

'Neither do you!'

I was beginning to get a little irritated by his seriousness.

I wanted him to lighten up so that we could do something more interesting than jumping up and down like a flat tennis ball.

'Look,' said the loblolly boy.

He reached up and undid the button at his neck. Then he held out his arms like a dancer and leapt into the air. My jaw dropped. Instead of falling immediately back down again, he seemed held up in the air momentarily as if attached to an invisible cord. And then he soared further, higher, until he had reached the height of the ancient tree. He levelled off then and swallow-dived over the little lake, rolling and barrelling in the air the way a porpoise spins in the ocean.

That was not the most wondrous thing, though. The most wondrous thing was that when he turned around I could see the spread of the feathery green wings that sprouted from his shoulders, beautiful waving wings.

He turned back and descended in a standing flight – arms outstretched, the wings clearly fanned behind him – and landed lightly before me.

'See,' he said. He was not even panting.

I felt as if I were suddenly on a different planet. Part of me wanted to drop to my knees. 'Who are you?' I gasped.

He shook his head slowly. 'I told you. I'm the loblolly boy,' he said.

We met again in the outer reaches of the Garden the next day, and the day following. I went along with the loblolly boy's insistence that I practise my silly little jumps. What I really wanted was to see him fly again. How could he have failed to see that all the practice in the world would not get me to fly? That I had an ordinary boy's shoulder blades – while he had amazing green wings.

He did let me touch the wings once. The feathers were long and soft and glittered in the dappled sunlight with a speckle and an emerald shine. They were beautiful. When he flexed his shoulders they lifted and stretched and I gasped at the lovely symmetry of them.

'No more,' I said. I had jumped about twenty times. I was getting better. I could reach nearly half my height from a standing leap. But now I was exhausted and annoyed by the uselessness of it.

'You have to really want to fly,' he said.

'You mean, I have to really want wings,' I said bitterly.

'I think,' he said, 'it's because you're self-conscious. It's too bright. You feel stupid.'

'You're right there,' I said. Who wouldn't feel a twit? Jumping up and down with my eyes squeezed shut like some hopeful yoyo. Saying to myself 'Fly! Fly! Fly!' What an idiot.

'It might be better to practise in the dark,' said the loblolly boy thoughtfully.

I shrugged. 'I can't see that it'd make much difference,' I said.

'I'll come and get you tonight,' he said. 'Where's your window?'

'How will you wake me?'

'I'll throw a stone,' he said.

'Don't you dare. You'll wake the whole building.'

I had to talk the loblolly boy out of throwing rocks against my window. He was so silly he'd have heaved one right through the glass and woken the whole place, including Mastiff, the biggest watchdog. Especially Mastiff the biggest watchdog.

'Just brush a branch back and forth against the pane,' I told him. 'The rustle will wake me up. I'm a light sleeper.'

'Are you sure?' he asked, his large green eyes wide with doubt. 'This is very important.'

'I'm sure,' I told him. 'Don't worry about it.'

The loblolly boy gave a little lopsided smile, and nodded. But I could see he was not convinced.

'I just don't want you to wake anybody else,' I added.

He shrugged. 'I could get away.'

I told you he was silly. 'You might be able to, but I can't,' I said.

———————

I'm not really brave. You're not allowed to be brave in the Great House. You put your head down and do as you're told. When the Keepers say 'Jump!' you jump. And when the Keepers say 'Quiet!' you don't say a word. And the Keepers hardly ever say anything else.

I was aware that the Keepers often seemed to pay special attention to me. This was probably because I didn't mix in with the others. They wanted you to mix in. They wanted to know where you were and what you were doing. I must have been a problem that way. And I looked different, too, with my red hair. The Keepers didn't like difference. I could sense that. I stood out.

16

Frightened as I was of the Keepers, though, I was more frightened of the watchdogs. I was especially terrified of Mastiff.

Mastiff was old and vicious. He wore a collar studded with spikes and had a jaw that was huge and square like a mechanical shovel. He panted like some kind of angry engine and white slobber dribbled down between the sharp teeth on either side of his black mouth. His eyes were small and mean and he always strained at the chain; so much so that the arm of his Keeper seemed unnaturally stretched. Whenever the watchdogs were disturbed in the night they set up a fearsome howling. The longest, most savage howl, I knew, came from Mastiff, the leader of the pack.

As I dropped down from the window beside the loblolly boy I felt as though the wall of the building was sliding down as well. I glanced up over my shoulder and realised with horror that the window was too high and the wall too smooth for me to get back inside again.

We raced away across the lawn and into the trees, but all I could think about was Mastiff: the gleaming teeth, the eyes shining with the thrill of the chase. I remembered with a lurch that the Keepers let the dogs off their leashes at night.

I was caught in a terrible dilemma. I wanted to run as fast as I could, but I knew that in doing so I would crash and thrash through the undergrowth and all that noise could alert the dogs and the Keepers. At the same time I was desperate to get as far away from the Great House as quickly as possible. In front of me the slender figure of the loblolly boy darted with effortless lightness this way, that way like a creature of the night. I realised that he was right: the Keepers and the watchdogs could never catch him, either on land or in the air.

They could catch me, though. I had no night vision. I could not dart or fly. I stumbled clumsily after the loblolly boy, agonising at every thud and snap I made.

Eventually, though, we made the spot where I'd practised so often. In the pale moonlight the little lake shone and the leafy tracery of the ancient tree was black against the stars. I fell to the ground, breathing harshly in short gasps.

'Do you really want to fly?' asked the loblolly boy.

'This is crazy,' I whispered.

He looked at me sadly in the moonlight.

'You have to want to!'

'How will I get back inside?' I demanded. 'I'll never climb back up that wall to the window.'

'Why would you want to?' he asked. 'If you could fly you'd just fly up over the great wall and never return. Why would you want to go back to that miserable dormitory?'

I stared at him. 'Because I do not have wings! I don't have any other choice. It is my home!'

I wanted to add, 'You egg!' but I probably didn't need to. He would know what I was feeling.

All the same, the loblolly boy did not seem to take offence. He just said softly, 'I guess, if I can't give you the desire to fly, something else will have to do the job . . .'

'What do you mean?'

He didn't reply. Instead he put two fingers to his mouth and let out a piercing whistle. Almost before the echo of the whistle faded from the wall across the water, I could hear the first, furious barrage of barking from the watchdogs.

I stared at him in horror.

'What have you done?' I whispered.

He didn't reply. He simply stood there waiting. Then his hand reached for mine.

Meanwhile the mad baying and barking of the dogs became louder and louder. And now I could hear human voices shouting and crying: the Keepers, following behind. But they would be following too far behind.

The dogs would be off their chains. I could see their gleaming eyes, their great chopping jaws opening and closing. Closer and closer. Now I could hear the snapping of the twigs and swish of foliage as they raced through the bushes.

'Hold my hand and jump!' said the loblolly boy.

I couldn't. I was frozen with fear.

The barking rose to a frenzied crescendo. I could see movement in the trees, dark shapes racing.

'Take my hand! Jump!' screamed the loblolly boy.

Blindly, I grabbed it. It was dry, yet somehow charged with energy. But the barking! I had to jump. I had to fly.

The first dog broke through the trees and leapt towards us. Mastiff. Face screwed up with savagery.

Just as he leapt towards me I leapt into the air. There was an arcing blue flash of electricity or something, and then to my amazement I saw the leaping dog's dark shape disappear beneath my feet. For a fraction of a second I could not understand it, and then in an amazing moment, I realised I was flying. I was really flying. I felt my shoulders lift, and beyond my shoulders I felt the great spread of my wings. I could feel them lift me up, up and up. Higher, higher, with a lightness I had never known before.

As they moved back and forth I could see their iridescent green in the moonlight, and to my astonishment I realised that I was no longer dressed in my baggy red overalls. My arms were covered in a fine sage-green material and my legs were green as well. Suddenly I realised what had happened.

I was a loblolly boy.

In the joy of it I swooped up and over and round and round. I laughed with delight as the cool air rushed through my hair and my wings. Not for long though, for even through the swish of the air I could hear the barking and shouting down below. I had forgotten the loblolly boy. Where was he?

I glanced to the left and right. I had no flying companion. I paused in mid-flight and stared down through the gloom. There were jumping shapes and dark figures all converged onto a single spot. I hovered down with wings outstretched.

The Keepers had arrived and were driving back the dogs with harsh shouts. One was holding a struggling figure up out of the animals' snapping jaws. A small figure in baggy red overalls. Even in the darkness I could see the basin-cut of dark red hair.

I realised instantly. I hovered above him. I didn't care.

'I told you!' he shouted.

I shook my head.

'Don't worry!' he cried. 'They can't see or hear you.'

I didn't care about that either. 'You changed us!'

'You're the loblolly boy now!' he cried.

'And you?'

'I'm real!' he laughed. 'I'm real!'

A Keeper, holding his struggling figure, clamped a hand over his mouth. 'Be quiet!' he shouted.

The figure did not say another word, and even stopped resisting as the party began to trudge back towards the Great House. I rose in confusion above the ancient tree until Keepers, dogs – now quiet – and the small figure disappeared beneath the leaves.

Far below me the little lake shone like a single sequin. I rose above it and glided towards the wall, looking over it for the first time. Immediately beyond was a great dark mass, peppered here and there with twinkling lights. The city I had not seen for years. Beyond the city was a vast, blacker expanse I thought was almost certainly the ocean. I rose even higher, glanced back at the solid cube that was the Great House, flexed my wings, then found an up-draught that lifted me further, higher, away from everything I had ever known.

TWO

THE OCEAN was more than I had ever imagined. I skirted the far-off city. He who had been the loblolly boy had suggested I couldn't be seen, but I didn't trust my invisibility yet, even in the darkness. I quickly exulted in the power of flight, but at the same time I was quite sure I did not want to draw attention to myself.

I learned to lean into the wind, and by extending my arms I discovered I could flex my wings. Like sails they would lift me higher. Then by drawing my elbows in I could lower them and I would fall in a gliding dive. Thus I could lift and fall at will. By leaning either way I could veer left or right. This all sounds, now, as if flying was something I was learning to do by trial and error. It was not that way at all, of course. If I had attempted to fly that way I would have tumbled from the sky with all the grace of a concrete mixer and about as quickly. No, as I had been born again as a loblolly boy, I seemed to have been born already flying.

From time to time, just as dawn was breaking, I tested myself by landing on some deserted spot: a hilltop, a rooftop of a lone house, the top of a macrocarpa tree. Each time I attempted to do so, I landed gracefully and elegantly, merely wobbling back and forth momentarily to steady myself, my wings folding in an instant back against my body, like those of a beetle. And once I was steady, and had looked about me to make sure I was alone, I leapt up into the air again, and found myself immediately in the arms of the breeze, rising higher and higher, swooping and soaring. It was wonderful.

Then the sky was lighter. The sun was rising over the sea's horizon. A great glow filled the heavens to the east and the clouds became red, then orange, then gold. I could see before me the vastness of the ocean stretching beyond the coastline. I had soared ever higher and I could see the dark scalloped pattern of rolling waves tumbling towards the shore and breaking into white horses. The coast at this point was hilly and deserted. To my left there was a plain and the far-off city, and there were sand hills dotted with pine trees. But where I found myself heading, the coastline was wild and rocky, rising to steep cliffs and bluffs and indented with small bays and coves. It was a strange thing, finding myself heading in a particular direction. I knew I was deliberately heading towards the cliffs and bluffs and not the sand hills, but I couldn't have told you why. It was as if I had no choice.

Not that I was thinking about it. I was so taken with the sheer delight of the air's buoyancy, the wonder of viewing the beauty of the world from such a cleansing height. It was as though the whole of the sky belonged to me, and this was a terrific feeling. I couldn't imagine why on earth the loblolly boy had tricked me into exchanging my fearful and imprisoned world for this. I shrugged and almost laughed at the stupidity of it. What on earth had he been thinking? There he was, seized roughly by the Keepers and their snarling hounds and frog-marched back to the dormitory and only God knew what punishments, while here was I, lord of the heavens, swooping and soaring in the greatest freedom I had ever known.

As I was exhilarating in this power I became aware I was not alone in my new element. Perhaps it was because I was closing in all the time on the coast that I eventually noticed the sky was dotted with birds: gulls, mostly, hovering lazily with outstretched wings on the sea breeze. If they were aware of me they did not show it. I remembered the loblolly boy hinting that he was invisible, and I wondered if the birds about me could see me at all.

To test the theory, I veered towards the nearest of these fellow creatures, a large black-backed gull quietly riding the morning breeze away to my left. It was magical to be able to approach the gull without it being in the remotest way aware of me. Within seconds I was flying alongside it, so close I could almost have touched its wing tips. The beautifully engineered white feathers of its head rippled slightly as the wind passed through them and its black eye was mildly taking in all that was below. The yellow beak was closed and I was near enough to see the nostril hole up there where the beak joined the head proper. The gull didn't glance my way at all. It was hovering so quietly – adjusting its wings by the tiniest fraction to attend to the demands of flying – that it could almost have been an astonishingly life-like model in some brilliant diorama.

However, I was wrong about my invisibility. Just when I thought I would test the theory even further by reaching out and actually stroking the outstretched wing, I heard a voice; a strange, disembodied voice that seemed to be coming from right inside my head.

Don't even think about it, loblolly boy. I don't want any of your silly games!

I was so startled by the voice that I lost balance, and I lurched most inelegantly down a metre or so, as if I had hit an air pocket. Awkwardly I had to scramble-fly up beside the gull once more.

'What?'

You heard me. Where have you been, anyway?

I stared, astonished, at the gull riding the sky silently beside me. As far as I'd been aware it hadn't so much as glanced at me. It had remained hovering there just as before. All the same there was that thin, high-pitched, inescapable voice in my head.

'Are you talking to me?' I whispered.

Of course I'm talking to you, said the voice. *How many other creatures do you see flying beside me at this moment?*

'But you're not even looking at me . . .' That sounded particularly pathetic. I knew that as soon as I'd whispered it. It would have been far more useful to have asked something like, *How are you talking to me? You're a black-backed gull!* You don't have conversations with black-backed gulls. Although, for that matter, you don't usually share air space with black-backed gulls either.

I didn't know why I was whispering. There was probably not another creature within twenty shouting distances, but

I was whispering as though I could have been overheard by the hills below.

I don't have to look at you to know you're there, loblolly boy.

'What do you mean, where have I been?' I asked.

Don't play the innocent with me. You've been up to your silly tricks again. He won't like it, you know.

'He?'

I told you not to do that. You're really impossible. I don't know why I bother sometimes!

I had apparently annoyed the gull, for it suddenly flapped its wings and swooped off to one side and fell down, down, down, growing smaller and smaller as it fell away.

I remained where I was. I lay on the up-draught as if I were floating in a blue lake. I was puzzled by what the gull had said, and a little concerned by the sound of the 'he' who wouldn't like it. It hadn't really occurred to me before that the loblolly boy would have connections and responsibilities. The flying thing had seemed such utter freedom, it was hard to imagine any constraints. So who was he? Did the loblolly boy have his own Keepers, his own wall? I suddenly realised with a sinking feeling how little I knew about the person I had become. Such a sinking feeling, indeed, that I found myself spiralling towards a small bay surrounded by tall cliffs.

As I dropped towards the bay I understood that this was where I had been heading all along. It was both unfamiliar and familiar at the same time. I had never been there before, I knew, but it was a place my whole being recognised as my destination.

I alighted on a small sand dune tufted with marram grass and gazed about me curiously.

✕

The bay was small: just a cove, really. There was a sandy beach of curiously black-and-silver sand between black basalt rocky outcrops. These outcrops were very rough and craggy, and kelp dangled over them where they met the sea. Perhaps because the bay was enclosed, the whole place had a salty tang with a whiff of iodine and fish. The beach ended in a small line of sand hills formed with the same black-and-silvery sand, and rising abruptly behind them was a towering cliff, dotted with hanging plants which had found some desperate purchase on the cliff wall. The cliff was splashed here and there with white where gulls or shags had nested on narrow ledges.

There was a road of sorts, although it was unsealed and I could see the line of grass that grew between the two shingled wheel tracks, which petered out in a small paddock. The cliffs were very steep, so that the road zigzagged down into the bay in a series of stretches and hairpin bends. There was no road out the other side, though. The only way you could get out of the bay from that side would be by rope ladder – by very, very long rope ladder. All the same, to the right there were three derelict little dwellings apparently built into caves at the base of the cliff. They were wooden and roofed with rusty corrugated iron. The first two had windows that had been clumsily boarded up, but the third had white curtains only half drawn. I gave a little start to see a thin spiral of smoke curling from a chimney built against the shore-side of the shack.

Somebody was at home!

Instinctively I stepped back. After my experience with the gull I was in no mood to test my invisibility. I fell to my knees and then lowered myself right down so that I was lying behind a large clump of marram grass. I drew the grass aside and peered through it, studying the shack carefully, looking especially for movement. There was none. The morning was silent and almost still. The only movement was that thin spiral of smoke rising until it caught a faint breeze.

I wondered about the shacks and who might live there. They looked old and run-down. They had probably been built with material brought in by boat. I guessed that nobody had lived in them for years and that the one nearest the sea was only used as a holiday place.

I rolled over and, lying on my back, stared up at the cliff towering before me and at the blue of the sky beyond. The events of the night and the morning were still not quite believable. Had I dreamed the whole thing? Had I really been given a new existence as a loblolly boy and taken to the air as a fish to water? Had I really flown in that wonderful blue? I closed my eyes and stared into the red as the sun shone through my eyelids. It was comforting. I felt soothed by it, the sand soft under my back. I realised that I was very tired, that I had not slept all night, that I had flown for miles and miles to get to this private little bay. I felt a drowsiness come upon me, and I welcomed it gently, and fell into a dreamless sleep.

'Do you love me?'

I was sure I was hearing a voice close by.

'Do you *really* love me?'

I was hearing a voice.

Opening my eyes, I rolled over onto my stomach and peered once more through the marram grass. Barely a metre away from me, lying on the sunny slopes of the sand hill, was a girl in a red-and-white-dotted bikini. She was rubbing coconut oil on her legs and I could smell the sweet, cloying scent. A boy was lying beside her with a sullen look on his face, sucking irritably on a stem of marram grass. I could not tell what expression the girl had on her face because her back was towards me. I could tell that she had long fair hair. I guessed that the pair were about sixteen, or perhaps a little older.

I glanced around. I had half expected to find that the loblolly boy and my flight over the wall had all been an amazing dream. But I had not woken up back in the Garden. I was still in the sunny little cove with the black-and-silver sand and the lapping sea.

I looked over towards the green paddock. There was no car there. How had this pair arrived? From nowhere. Had they flown in like me? Dropped down from the brilliant blue sky?

Whether the boy loved the girl or not, he was apparently not prepared to say. He turned away from her and stared out to sea. Following his glance, I could see a small sailing dinghy pulled up on the sand. That explained their presence.

What was not explained was why they had chosen to sunbathe just centimetres from where I was sleeping. Surely they would have seen me as they'd walked up the sand hill to find a place to spread their large red beach towels and plonk their big wicker picnic hamper. Unless the loblolly boy had been right and . . .

Acting on a sudden whim, I stood up. If they were going to see me, they would surely see me now.

I was completely ignored. They clearly couldn't see me at all. The girl lay back down. I looked at her, trying to gauge her mood. It was difficult because she was wearing those sunglasses with mirror lenses. I stepped towards her and leaned over her. I could not see myself in the mirrors. As if to confirm my invisibility, the boy turned towards her again. I may as well have not been there.

'Well?'

The boy's lack of response was clearly irritating her.

Eventually he spoke, although he turned away from her once more and was again staring out to sea.

'I don't see how pinching stuff from one of those cottages proves that I love you. I don't see how it proves anything at all, really.'

'It proves you're a wimp if you won't,' she said, sniffing slightly as if she had a bad smell in her nostrils.

'What's being a wimp got to do with it? Who says I'm a wimp?'

'If you loved me you'd get me that telescope.'

'What telescope?'

'Don't be silly. You know what telescope.'

'I do not.'

'The one we saw when we looked through the window.'

'I didn't see any telescope.'

'You did so. The one on the mantelpiece. The brass one.'

'I'm not a wimp.'

'You are!'

'I'll prove it.' He stood up and dusted sand off his shorts. He looked towards the cliff. 'I'll climb that cliff. That'll prove it.'

She turned and stared straight through me. She shrugged. 'I don't want you to climb that stupid cliff. I want you to get me that telescope.'

'If you want it so much, why don't you get it yourself?'

'I want you to get it. I want you to prove you love me . . .'

'I can't just walk into somebody's house and pinch a telescope off their mantelpiece!'

'It's nobody's house.'

'It is so somebody's house. Look, there's smoke coming from the chimney, for goodness' sake.'

'Well, there's nobody home.'

'How do you know that?'

'Did we see anybody?'

'So?'

'So there's nobody home. Probably out fishing or something.'

'How do you know that?'

'You're beginning to sound like a stuck record. If you're not man enough to get it for me, just say so.'

'I suppose you realise that *just getting it for you* is stealing.'

'It's not really.'

'How so?'

'Nobody really owns those shacks. They've been there for

years. Whoever lit that fire wouldn't live there, for goodness' sake. Work it out. Where's the nearest supermarket?'

'So?'

'So, finders keepers. Okay?'

The boy slumped into a morose silence once more. The girl lay back and looked as though she was going to sleep. I guessed her eyes were closed behind her mirror glasses. The boy glanced towards her again and seemed to soften. He reached towards her and tenderly touched her outstretched fingertips.

Instantly she flinched. 'Don't touch me!'

'What's the matter with you?'

'I just don't want you to touch me, that's all.'

'Bloody hell!'

'You don't love me . . .'

'I do. You know I do . . .'

'Then prove it.'

'This is crazy.'

'No it's not. It's a test. A simple test. A quest, if you like. You know, like the knights and their . . . what were they?'

'Horses? Maidens? Damsels?'

'Yeah, damsels.'

'So, as far you're concerned that telescope is . . .'

'The Holy Grail. Right.'

The boy sighed. 'You're crazy. You know that? Quite crazy.'

'Yeah,' she said. 'I'm bananas. And I want that telescope. I want to look at the world through it. I want to look at you through it.'

'Do you?'

'Right.'

He sighed again, and began idly drawing circles in the sand. 'You know, Veronica, you drive a very hard bargain.'

'That's me,' said the girl sharply. 'And if you knew anything about me at all, Jason, you'd be on your bike and getting me that telescope right now!'

At that point I left them. I could sense that this bickering conversation could go on for quite a while. Besides, they'd made me curious about this precious telescope. Now that I was reassured about my invisibility I was more relaxed about wandering along the beach to the three shacks.

I thought I'd have a look in the windows. I also had a thought that somehow I could fly up and see if I could find the person or persons who lived there. I could do a good Samaritan act and somehow warn them that a burglary was being planned.

It didn't take me long to make my way across the little beach. As I'd suspected, the first shack was derelict. Nobody had lived there for a long time. The second shack was equally run-down, but the third shack was in a good enough state of repair, although the iron was rusty and the woodwork looked as though it needed a good coat of paint. The windows, as I'd noticed from the sand dune, were closed, but they were not boarded up and I could see ancient white curtains hanging in lacy tatters on the inside.

There was no sound. No radio. No movement of any kind, but there was that curl of smoke rising from the chimney. Now that I was closer I could smell the sweetish wood-smoke aroma, and I saw a great pile of bleached driftwood somebody had gathered and left in an untidy pile near the front door.

I glanced back over my shoulder. In the distance I could see the girl, Veronica, still sunning herself and Jason still sitting beside her, arms clasped about his knees and staring my way. For the hell of it, I waved at him, but he made no response. I was, it seemed, still quite invisible.

This made me a little bolder, so I stepped up to the nearest window and peered into the gloomy interior. I was eager to see this telescope that Veronica was so keen to get her hands on.

THREE

THERE IT WAS. Suddenly I knew why Veronica had so desperately wanted it. I don't know what I was expecting – a small tarnished object perhaps – but this telescope was neither small nor tarnished. It was tall and polished to a high gleam, like a brand-new trumpet in a brass band. It stood proudly on the wooden mantelpiece of the small brick fireplace. Cylinder within cylinder within cylinder. I could also understand her boyfriend's hesitation. This was a precious object. It had a sense of belonging. There was no possible finders-keepers rule that could excuse stealing it. This was really a holy grail and I somehow understood that stealing it would incur a terrible penalty.

And suddenly there was another reason why the boyfriend should have been nervous. I had been so taken with the telescope I had not realised that the room, which seemed to be a kitchen cum bed-sitting room, was occupied. Sitting near the fire in a rocking chair was an old man in a vaguely nautical uniform. He was knitting.

It was odd I hadn't noticed him coming into the house.

The girl in the spotted bikini had said the shack was empty. There did not seem to be any other room. How come they hadn't seen him?

Secure in my invisibility, I studied him. He did look very old, although I had not had a lot of experience of very old people. His hair, underneath a nondescript officer's cap with a single anchor for a badge, was long and white. His fingers, manipulating the knitting needles skilfully, were gnarled and blotched and his face was ruddy and weathered. It looked like a face that had seen a vast number of storms in a vast number of oceans. He was wearing gold-rimmed glasses perched on the end of his nose. They had small round lenses.

He seemed to become aware that he was being watched and he looked up swiftly and gazed at the window through which I was staring so brazenly. His eyes were a pale blue and it seemed impossible he couldn't see me. There was such an air of authority about him, I had to admit I was glad he couldn't.

As I had with the boyfriend a few moments previously, I raised my hand and waved at him through the window, although with only half the confidence I had been feeling earlier.

With good reason, as it happened.

To my shock, he waved back and then abruptly stood up and marched to the door.

'You silly loblolly boy! Come in. Come in!' he ordered, standing at the open door. I now realised how tall he was: so tall he had to stoop in the doorway. I looked up at him and swallowed, gave a weak little smile and hurried into the shack with one last look over my shoulder, towards the dunes. If the young couple had noticed the flurry of movement, had seen the tall old man, and the door opening and closing, they gave no sign of it.

'Where have you been, little one?' the old man asked. His words seemed kindly enough although the tone was brusque. 'The gull told me he'd seen you.'

The gull?

How did this old man know I was a loblolly boy? How, if it came to that, could he see me? Gull? He could only have meant the gull I had flown beside before I came down into this little bay.

'What's the matter?' he asked. 'Cat got your tongue?'

He stared at me more fixedly and I looked away, made shy by the intensity of his stare. He seemed to be the sort of man who could find out whatever there was to know about you simply by looking closely. Before I turned away, though, I'd had time to notice his pale-blue eyes widen in sudden concern.

Then he was at the window, drawing the lacy curtains aside to let in more light. And then he was back by my side, holding me by my arms. He forced me around so that I was facing him. I looked up guiltily, as if I had done something wrong, had stolen something valuable. Something like the telescope.

'My, my, my,' the old man murmured.

I forced myself to look at him again. His cap was set at an angle and his eyebrows were bushy and white. There was an odour about him of salt, sandalwood and blue smoke, and his voice had a strange accent: not foreign exactly, but of far-off times and unimagined ships that had sunk to the bottom of the seas in ages past.

'My, my,' he repeated. 'I do believe you're a Newborn . . .'

'A Newborn?' I faltered.

'Tell me,' said the old man. 'Have you ever been in this little house before?'

'No,' I said. 'Of course not. How could I? I've never even been in this bay before.'

That was true. They didn't let you out of the Great House to go on visits, especially not to pretty little bays like this. He said nothing for some moments, then he let go of my arms and led me to a small easychair. 'Sit down,' he said. 'I think you'd better tell me all about it.'

So I did. I told him all about the Great House and the Keepers and Mastiff, all about the Garden and the Great Wall. I told him about how I'd met the loblolly boy in the Garden and how he had taught me to fly by forcing the issue, by making me want to fly more than anything in the world as I heard Mastiff's furious barking and imagined the slaver of his evil jaws.

I told him how I had seen the Keepers seize the little figure of the loblolly boy far below me, the loblolly boy who now had my red hair and looked just as I had done, and how I had grown wings and was able to soar with wonder into the freedom of the night sky.

The old man nodded from time to time, as if my story were not in the least unusual, as if exchanging bodies and being able to fly were quite normal, and as if talking to black-backed gulls and being invisible were everyday occurrences.

When I had finished, he took my hand and held it gravely for some moments.

'I was right,' he said. 'You are a Newborn. I suppose I should welcome you to the Cove.'

He didn't sound too happy about what had happened, though. It was almost as though something terrible had happened to me.

'What is a Newborn?' I asked.

'What you are. What has happened to you. You have been born anew as the loblolly boy and he who was the loblolly boy has escaped into the real world again.'

I looked about me. At the comfortable room with its iron bed and patchwork quilt, at the square oak table and three battered chairs, at the rocking chair by the fire, and at the fireplace itself, with the gleaming telescope and a pipe rack on its mantelpiece. I glanced out of the window at the sea beyond, the steep heads of the little bay and the blue sky dotted with wheeling gulls. It all looked like the world to me.

'But I am in the world,' I said.

'Are you?' asked the old man gently.

'Of course I am,' I said stubbornly.

The old man walked across to the window and stared towards the sand dunes where the couple were still sunbathing. 'Those young ones out there,' he said. 'Are they in the real world?'

'Of course!' I said.

'You were with them for some time?'

'Yes, I was. I listened to their conversation . . .' I stared at the old man, remembering. 'Yes, I did. And they were planning to steal your telescope,' I said excitedly. 'At least the girl was. She was trying to persuade her boyfriend to do it. She was using all sorts of crazy blackmail. I think it was working. That's why I came over here, to . . .'

This didn't seem to bother the old man a whit. 'So when you were with them, did they talk to you?'

'Of course not,' I said. 'I was . . . I was sort of invisible.'

'I see,' said the old man gently. 'You were sort of invisible?'

I nodded.

'So as far as those people in the dunes were concerned, you were not there at all.'

I thought about that. 'I suppose so, but I *was* there . . .'

'Were you?'

This was going round in circles. 'Of course I was.'

'But tomorrow, if anybody asks that pair what they saw and who they met in this cove, neither of them will mention you. As far as they are concerned you do not exist.'

'But I *do* exist!' I said angrily. 'I'm here, aren't I?'

He shook his head sadly. 'But *where* do you exist? Are they in the real world, or are you?'

I stared at him. This was too difficult. Then I saw a way out of the circle. 'But,' I said triumphantly, '*you* can see me. *You* saw me as soon as I looked in your window!'

The old man shook his head again. 'Of course I can see you. All that means is that we are in the same world, not . . .'

I stared at him in horror. I knew what he was going to say. He was going to say *not in the real world*. I should have

40

realised this a long time ago. I was the one who'd thought the loblolly boy was stupid. But I was the stupid one all along.

'Who are you?' I whispered.

He smiled sadly. 'I am the captain,' he said. 'My name is Captain Bass. I live here in this small bay and from time to time I'm able to offer solace and comfort to people like you, people who find themselves tricked out of their real existences. Don't look so alarmed, little loblolly boy. I'll do what I can for you. It may not be much. It may be something . . .'

Just at that moment, I caught a movement at the window. I glanced towards it, and the captain, seeing me turn, glanced too. There was Jason behind the glass, staring nervously through the window at the telescope.

It looked like Veronica had got her way after all.

'Can he see us?' I whispered.

The captain shook his head. 'No he can't. He can only see what he wants to see.'

'The telescope?'

The captain nodded. 'I'm afraid so.'

'Should we lock the door?'

The captain shook his head sadly. 'There would be no point. He is on a quest. He must have the telescope.'

'But,' I said, 'he can't have the telescope, can he?'

'Oh no,' said the captain. 'He can't have the telescope. You're learning fast, little loblolly boy.'

'What will happen?' I asked.

'What will happen is what must happen,' said the captain.

41

At that point there was a rattle at the door. Jason had worked up enough courage to twist the handle. We waited silently. I saw the wooden ball of the door handle turn, and the door was pushed inwards with an apprehensive creak.

Moments later, the boy named Jason stepped cautiously into the room. As if the floor were red-hot, he stepped across the bare white boards, the ragged mat, until he reached the fireplace. All the time he was glancing nervously back and forth as if he had some twitchy built-in radar.

The huge figure of Captain Bass was sitting in his rocking chair. I was sitting on the edge of the iron bed. Quite clearly, Jason could see neither of us, had no idea we were in the room watching his every move. I was at a loss to know what the captain would do. I did remember that his words had sounded so ominous that I had felt a momentary chill. *He can't have the telescope.* Despite his words, though, the captain had made no attempt to prevent Jason from seizing the instrument. Instead, he seemed to be almost willing him to take it.

Jason acceded. He reached for the telescope.

As soon as the telescope was in Jason's grip, however, the captain spoke in a deep voice that seemed to fill, then reverberate around, the room.

Now that you have the telescope, why don't you look through it?

If Jason was startled by the sudden disembodied voice, he gave no indication. He simply muttered, 'Good idea,' and, stepping back from the fireplace, lifted the telescope to his right eye, closing his left into a squint as he did so. Then he swung around the room, manoeuvring the telescope up and down as if trying to focus on every single object: the hanging oil lamps, the dusty pots above the wood stove, the model square-rigger in the glass case. He even trained the telescope directly on me at one point, moving it up and down the patchwork quilt.

What do you see? asked the captain's deep voice once more.

'This is seriously weird, man,' he muttered. 'No matter where I look with this damn thing, all I can see is a big brown seal sitting on a rock.'

He lowered the telescope and rubbed at his eye vigorously. Then he put the telescope to his eye again.

'Same old stupid seal,' he muttered. 'Why does the thing only let me see a seal when there's no seal anywhere?'

He took the telescope away from his eye again, looking about him in frustration. 'What sort of a telescope is this anyway? Idiot Veronica.'

It's a special telescope, boomed the voice of Captain Bass. *A very special telescope. It doesn't bring things closer in space, it brings things closer in time . . .*

'That doesn't make sense,' said Jason. 'Brings things closer in time?'

It allows you to see the future, boomed the voice.

'The future? That's ridiculous. What future? All there is, is a stupid seal!'

Your future, boomed Captain Bass. *Step outside and see!*

'Bloody Veronica . . .' muttered Jason. It didn't seem to occur to him that he'd been discussing things with a voice coming from thin air. Neither did he seem to think that he should do anything other than follow instructions.

Accordingly, he placed the telescope back on the mantelpiece and moved towards the door. I was curious, so I stood up off the bed and followed him. Jason swung the door open and stepped outside, slamming it in my face.

I opened the door, and to my astonishment, instead of Jason's departing back, there was a large brown seal sitting on the black boulders just beyond the door. The seal turned and looked back over its shoulder at the shack. 'Arf! Arf!' it barked despondently, its whiskers hanging in unhappy arcs on either side of its nose.

I turned around to face Captain Bass. 'Is that . . .?' I asked with wonder.

He nodded.

'You knew that was going to happen?'

He stood up and came to the door as well and, stooping, stepped outside. He stared at the mournful seal impassively for some moments, then he waved at it with his fingers. 'Shoo! Shoo!' he said. 'Go and find yourself some fish!'

'You knew it was going to happen?' I repeated.

'Oh, yes,' said Captain Bass. 'As soon as he said that a seal was all he could see, I knew that being a seal was going to be his future.'

The seal had flopped forward a few miserable metres, then stopped and looked back at the shack again.

'Shoo!' the captain said once more, a little more forcefully.

'He looks so desperately upset. Can't you change him back again? I'm sure he's learnt his lesson.'

The captain turned to me. 'Me? What made you think it was *me*? I don't have that sort of power. The power was in

44

the telescope. I didn't ask him to take it up. The telescope understood what he was up to and responded accordingly.'

I turned with horror back to the seal. It seemed to have given up all hope of help coming from the shack and was now flopping awkwardly over the rocks towards the sea. 'He'll stay like that . . .'

'Forever,' completed Captain Bass, matter-of-factly.

'But that's terrible,' I protested. 'Terrible,' I whispered.

'I don't know that it's that terrible,' said the captain. 'After all, he's just exchanged one existence for another. He'll probably quite enjoy being a seal. It's not a bad life, really. You get to bask a lot on the rocks, you don't really feel the cold, and you get to swim as much as you want. Plenty of fish to eat. He'll probably get to quite enjoy it.'

The seal that had been Jason had now reached the water's edge, but seemed somewhat reluctant to go in. Instead he backed away again, looking disconsolately over his shoulder.

'He'll probably take to swimming as easily as you took to flying,' remarked the captain, giving me a meaningful glance. The full significance of what the captain had said suddenly sank in and I shuddered. It was true. I had taken to flying. And I had loved it. I had changed existences, too. I was now something called a loblolly boy. I had been a boy. Jason, who had also been a boy, was now a seal. And the captain said that Jason would be a seal forever. And that meant . . .

I did not want to think about that. I glanced towards the sand dune. Veronica had stood up and was shading her eyes to look over at the cottage. She was clearly looking for Jason. She continued to stare for some time and then, shrugging angrily, gathered a towel about her shoulders and began to walk purposefully towards us.

When she was a few metres away she shouted, 'Jason!'

There was of course no reply. The door of the shack was now open; I was standing before it and the captain was standing beside it. It was clear that Veronica was not able to see either of us.

'Jason!'

At her second shout, the seal barked. I turned to look at it and saw that it was flopping awkwardly back over the rocks towards the shack.

'Arf! Arf! Arf!'

Veronica, who had been hurrying towards the open door of the shack, stopped at the sound and looked at the approaching seal uncertainly. Then she began to back off, shouting, 'Go away! Go away!'

This time the seal stopped uncertainly. It raised itself on to its front flippers and lifted its head into the air, moving it from side to side and whimpering piteously.

'Get off!' screamed Veronica, emboldened by the seal's confusion. She bent down and grabbed a large stick of driftwood and flung it angrily at the seal. She was a terrible shot and the stick flew harmlessly over the seal's back. The seal whimpered again and retreated a few feet. Then it barked again.

Veronica became even bolder. She bent over again and this time found a rock. She drew her arm back and let go. This time she did hit the seal. The rock thwacked into its flank and it yelped with pain then turned and flopped in a panic towards the sea.

'Stupid thing!' hissed Veronica. Then she looked up and about her again. 'Jason! Where are you! Jason! I've just been attacked by a crazy seal!'

She paused, but there was no response. Then she shrugged petulantly once more and strode towards the shack. She reached the open doorway and stared inside.

'Jason?'

When she had ascertained that there was no Jason inside the hut, she paused. 'Odd . . .' she whispered.

She stepped into the shack and Captain Bass stepped in after her, signalling me to come too. What happened next was, I suppose, inevitable. I would have tried to stop the silly girl, but I didn't know how. In an instant she saw the telescope still standing on the mantelpiece and she marched towards it and grabbed it. 'What a wimp,' she said bitterly. 'He's probably off hiding somewhere preparing some cock-and-bull story about how the shack was locked or something. Pathetic.'

She lifted the telescope to her eye and stared through it. Immediately she brought it down again.

'That's funny,' she muttered. 'How come all I can see is that stupid seal? I'm not looking out the door or the window.'

She tried again, and just as quickly brought the telescope down again.

'Must be something wrong with it.'

Have a look outside! suggested Captain Bass in his ringing tones.

Just as Jason had accepted the voice without question, so did Veronica. 'Good idea,' she whispered. 'Might be something to do with the light . . .'

47

Tucking the telescope under one arm, she stepped outside again. Although I was watching carefully, the transformation was instantaneous. One moment there was a fair-haired girl in a dotted bikini wrapped about with a red towel; the next moment there was a large brown fur seal yelping in astonishment. I could not for the life of me tell when the girl ended and the seal began.

The other seal, meanwhile, had gathered enough courage to approach the shack once more. Perhaps he had sensed what was going to happen. For a moment or two both animals, propped on their fore-flippers, stared at each other, then the seal that had been Veronica gave an agonised bark and lurched over the rocks towards the seal that had been Jason. He did not wait for her. He turned as she began to move, and trundled awkwardly towards the sea. This time he did not pause at the water's edge, but moved quickly and increasingly smoothly into the sea and within seconds had disappeared from view. The other seal, as if desperate to catch him, followed in a barking panic and splashed into the sea as well.

Captain Bass leant over and picked up the shiny brass telescope lying on the ground near the door to the shack. It had fallen there when Veronica's arm had turned into a flipper. He checked it briefly for damage then grunted with satisfaction.

'Well, I think that is that,' he remarked. 'I'll put this back on the mantelpiece. It's seen enough excitement for one day.'

I looked at him sharply. It seemed to me that Captain Bass had a remarkably cold view of the world. I was almost shaking with the shock of what had happened to Jason and Veronica; Captain Bass was treating the whole thing as if they had climbed onto a bus and driven off to the movies or something.

The captain paused in the doorway and looked back at me. His eyes were very old.

'Don't take it so hard, loblolly boy,' he said. 'These things happen.'

I nodded, but I didn't feel like nodding.

'Come inside now,' he said, brandishing the telescope. 'And I hope you've seen what can happen if you bite off more than you can chew!'

I thought that was a little uncalled for. Hadn't I been changed into a loblolly boy? It seemed I'd already bitten off far more than I'd realised.

FOUR

THE CAPTAIN made himself a lunch of bacon and eggs and fried bread, but made no effort to feed me. In fact, he offered me not so much as a glass of water. He finished off his own meal with a tankard of black home-brewed stout. The sound and smells of his lunch filled the small living room: fried bacon, spitting fatty and salty; fried eggs, crackling; and the dark, yeasty froth and bubble of the stout. The air was rich with these smells but, strangely, they did not stir my appetite. In fact, I realised with a pang of regret that I didn't have an appetite. Not at all. It had apparently gone the way of my red hair.

The captain dug into his meal with relish. He was not a tidy eater; quite the reverse. The bare wooden table was quickly flecked with grease spots and gobbets of food, as were the ends of his draggling moustache and bushy white beard. He was also very noisy. He sucked and slurped and splashed with huge enjoyment. When he finished he stood up and let out a tremendous belch. Then he rubbed his eyes vigorously. He told me that he always had a 'postprandial nap'. That meant, he explained, a little sleep after his food.

He stared at me meaningfully and told me I'd better not make any disturbing noises for an hour or so or he'd 'get the telescope' onto me.

Almost immediately he lay down on his iron bed and pulled the patchwork quilt over himself. The bed was quite a large one, but the captain made it look tiny.

The captain's sleeping was just as noisy as his eating. He sighed and gasped, snorted and snored, and every so often would whimper strange words in a variety of languages.

I wondered about the appetite thing. It had not occurred to me that being a loblolly boy meant I might never eat food again. It was a dreadful thought. No ice-cream, fresh plums from the fridge, Marmite sandwiches with chopped walnuts, fish and chips – all the things I'd dreamed about in my dorm in the Great House where we'd been given spaghetti mince and semolina every night of the week.

I had to give a little grin, though, at the captain's telling me to be quiet when, within a short time, he began making enough noise to bring the iron roof down. In fact it wasn't long before the captain's shouting, whimpering and snoring drove me out of the shack and onto the sands of the bay.

A wind sprang up and it blew through the filmy green clothes I was wearing. I supposed the weather was cool, I supposed I should have been cold, but somehow I was beyond temperature. I remembered how I had flown through the end of the night and the early morning. I'd been hundreds of metres up in the air but I hadn't noticed that it was particularly cold. And then when Veronica and Jason had been sunbathing I hadn't noticed it being especially warm.

To test the theory I leapt into the air again and rose above the bay, above the cliffs, rising higher and higher. Eventually I climbed far above the highest bird. Looking down, I could see the little cave dwellings grow tinier and tinier and then disappear into a haze, while rivers and roads beyond the hills narrowed into thinner and thinner lines until they disappeared. The city gathered into itself until it was merely a dark smudge. And yet, I felt no chill. I must have been higher than the highest mountain in the land, higher than Everest even, but I felt no colder than I had down on the little beach.

Thoughtfully, I flew down again in great swooping arcs. I should have been getting warmer, but there was no difference.

What had I become? A Newborn, the old man had called me. But born into what? I remembered his expression of sadness and concern. Suddenly, I felt a chill: not a chill on my body, but a chill in my heart. Perhaps being a loblolly boy was not something wonderful at all.

Perhaps it was something terrible.

Now, sitting on the rocks of the bay with Captain Bass, I was about to find out.

'There are certain things,' announced Captain Bass, 'that a Newborn must learn.'

It was late afternoon and we had left the little shack and were sitting on a large rock to the south of the bay. The sea glittered before us in the late-afternoon sun. I looked about the water for the seals, but they were nowhere to be seen.

'At first,' said the captain, 'you would have found the experience of flight quite exhilarating.'

I nodded, remembering.

'It was,' I said. 'It was wonderful. It still is. Partly it was because I was able to escape the Great House and the Keepers and the dogs and all that.'

'Aye,' said the captain. 'Folk often forget that when they are desperate to escape *from* something they have to escape *into* something else.'

I knew what he meant. I knew the old saying about the frying pan and the fire.

'And then, there is the invisibility. How wonderful. I guess everybody would like to be invisible.'

I nodded again. I remembered all the times when I would have loved to be invisible. Those times when the Tutors in the Great House had humiliated me by asking questions I had no idea about.

'What a Newborn, what all Newborns, must come to realise,' continued the old man, 'is that while there is an initial thrill and exhilaration in the flying and in the invisibility, this quickly palls. It is wonderful, but it comes at a terrible price. You see, the trade-off is the loss of human contact. There is a certain wicked thrill in being able to stand beside people and listen to their conversations knowing you can't be seen. But you can't be heard either, or touched or sensed in any way, and so there is no way you can communicate with anybody. You're completely cut off . . .'

I began to see what the old man was getting at. I remembered being so close to Jason and Veronica, and yet they were totally unaware of my presence. As far as they were concerned I simply wasn't there. Then I remembered yet another thing. I had walked away from them across the black-and-silver sand. The sand was soft, warm and silky, but . . .

'I didn't leave any footprints,' I whispered.

The captain understood immediately. He nodded sadly. 'Yes, no footprints. Real people need to leave footprints. It's a comfort, a reassurance that they are part of the world. A reassurance a loblolly boy doesn't have.'

'That means,' I said, 'it's like a movie . . . that the real world, this world, is nothing more to me than a movie. I can watch it and hear it but I'm not part of it!'

'No,' said the old man. 'You're not.'

'It's sort of like being dead,' I whispered. 'Like being a ghost . . .'

He nodded again. 'Perhaps. Perhaps it's more like a dream from which you can never awaken . . .'

I began to understand why the loblolly boy had been so willing to Exchange with me. But then, at the thought of him, I saw something wrong in Captain Bass's depressing description of my life as a loblolly boy. My loblolly boy had spoken to me, hadn't he? I had been able to see him, hear him, touch him . . . I saw the possibility of escape after all.

'But you *can* be seen!' I said. 'The loblolly boy spoke to me. I could see him and hear him. He came to my window and woke me up!'

The old man sighed. 'I know. I know.'

'But how could that happen?' I demanded.

The captain adjusted his cap and didn't answer for a while. 'In your travels,' he said, 'from time to time you will come across people who *can* see you and who *can* speak to you. We call such people *Sensitives*. Some will be like the boy you were: young, innocent and harmless; some will be like me: old and not really of the world ourselves. We will be kindly enough disposed towards you. But then there are others who will not be so kindly disposed towards you. Who, to be blunt, will be very dangerous.'

I waited. I did not like the sound of this.

'It may be that you'll come across very few of these people, and I pray especially that you don't come across any of the third type. These are the Collectors: they'll see you as a rare and exotic species and they'll want to keep you in a cage or in a tank like some snow leopard or rare marmoset; then there are the Researchers: they'll want to analyse you. Take you to pieces. Find out by the process of dissection just how your system works. I needn't talk about the Trophy Hunters or the Inquisitors, or the Invigilators or the Investigators . . .'

I shuddered. 'How will I recognise these people?' I asked.

The old man shrugged. 'I have no idea,' he said. 'But I do strongly suggest you recognise them before they recognise you . . .'

'But what about the Sensitives?'

I was keen to hear about the Sensitives. It seemed to me that they offered the only hope out of this mess. If I could come across one of these and Exchange with them . . .

The captain looked at me gravely again with his old, old eyes. He knew exactly what I was thinking.

'Yes, little loblolly boy, you could. You could find such a person, work yourself into their trust, and effect an Exchange, but then what? You would be another person, living in the real world again. But you would not be the person you were. You would have stolen another's life. That's what you would have done. Worse than that, you would have condemned that person to the living death of being a loblolly boy . . . Are you prepared to be a murderer, little loblolly boy? Are you prepared to do that?'

I stared at him with a growing despair. 'But it's not fair,' I protested. 'How can I . . .'

'Of course it's not fair,' said the old man. He turned away and looked out to sea once more. The late afternoon sun glittered on the ocean. Near the shore, black rocks wrapped about with the sway of bull kelp and the surging splash of waves shouldered their way through to the surface. Suddenly, near one of the closer rocks, a brown head emerged, and then another. 'Look!' said Captain Bass, pointing. 'There they are.'

There were the two seals. They were sporting in the water. Diving and surfacing. They were dangerously close to the rocks, I thought, until I realised that the sea and the rocks were their element now. As the air was mine. They looked as if they'd always been part of the scene.

'They seem to have adjusted to their new life quite well,' grunted the captain, standing up. 'A good thing, too.' He gave me a meaningful glance, and I understood that he was not only talking about the seals.

><

I spent the next few days in the little cove trying to come to grips with my new life. I could have stayed in the captain's shack, I suppose, but I quickly realised I didn't have to worry about shelter any more. Because I didn't eat, there was no need to trouble the captain for food or drink, and because I no longer felt the cold there was no need for the warmth of a bed. I found it was just as comfortable, preferable in fact, to find a spot on a sand dune and sleep under the stars and the great yellow moon. Besides, the captain often frightened me with his ancient eyes and his gruff way of speaking. His noises would not have allowed me any rest either: his snorts and belches and snores, his splutters, coughing and hacks.

It was far better to keep my distance. To approach the captain warily from time to time and check out his mood before trying to find out more of my strange new existence. When he was in a good mood he was quite useful in this regard, telling me more about the Collectors who would set great value on adding me to their glass cases. To these horrible people, I was apparently like an unused Penny Black or some other really rare stamp to a stamp collector. They would risk anything to add a loblolly boy to their collection.

But when the captain was in a grumpy mood he was difficult and would often threaten me with the telescope if I didn't stop being a nuisance. I never felt I was being a nuisance, but at that threat I always made myself scarce: I had seen what the telescope had done to Jason and Veronica. It was weird enough being a loblolly boy without being changed into a dung beetle or a sand flea or something nasty like that.

All the same, I did begin to think about the telescope. As the days bled into each other and as I realised that the only human contact I had at all was with the bad-tempered, old and unpredictable Captain Bass, I began to wonder more and more about the future. Was this all I had to look forward to? A life sleeping on a sand dune under the stars and a yellow moon? Never speaking to anybody real, never talking to anybody real, never having anybody real pass the time of day with me? I even began to miss some of the people back at the Great House. Not the other kids in the dorm, though. I was only too pleased to be free of them. They all treated the bottom of the pile like some sort of a football: an opportunity for free kicks. And I had always seemed to be at the bottom of the pile. But the Matron and the Tutors had only been really awful some of the time. I even began to miss the Keepers. They were pretty hard, but every once in a while if you weren't breaking the rules they might bark 'Hi' or 'Nice day' or something like that.

I began to fret. Was I doomed to stay in this little cove forever, or was I going to fly high into the sky once more and wing my way to some other place? Would some other place be any better? If I left this bay and its increasingly boring safety, would I be putting myself in danger from the Collectors or the Researchers or the Invigilators or whatever they were called?

The more I thought about these things, the more I thought about the telescope. It seemed to me that it could almost certainly tell me the answers.

And so it happened that on the occasions when I went into his shack to say hello to Captain Bass, I would often steal a glance at the mantelpiece and the brass tubes of the telescope sitting there. I began to picture myself holding it to my eye and training it on the future. What would it reveal? I began to wish the captain elsewhere. I began to will him outside, with his vile pipe and his fishing rod, to leave me alone with the telescope. But somehow he seemed to sense this. He'd perhaps look my way and find my wistful gaze on the telescope and he'd 'Harrumph' and ask me some irritating question. It was quite clear to me that he understood my growing need and was doing everything in his power to deflect it. I guess this should have warned me, should have told me that the old man had my best interests at heart; but all it did was make me more determined to seize the opportunity when it arose, to grab the telescope and put it to my eye. Even the lesson of Jason and Veronica was fading. From time to time I would see the pair of them frolicking in the waves or basking on a black rock and it no longer felt as though they'd lost out on the deal. Being a seal might not be too bad after all, I managed to convince myself.

And then the opportunity did present itself.

One morning I rose high into the sky to stretch my powers of flight. It was a beautiful morning. The sea glittered below like an aquamarine coverlet and the huddling hills closed protectively about the little bay. In a way it was good to flex my wings again. I could feel them adjusting to the breeze quite independently of any conscious control on my part. Flying, it seemed, was as automatic as breathing. Far, far below me I could see the three cave houses: the two deserted ones and the captain's, closest to the heads. I soared there lazily, riding the up-draughts, and as I was doing so I noticed a tiny figure moving purposefully along the narrow path that followed the hillside above the rocky shore. It was Captain Bass. I swooped down and saw that he was carrying an old sugar bag in one hand and a fishing rod in the other. I knew where he was going. He was heading out towards the point where there were some large rocks and he would fish there for the butterfish that fed below the kelp. It was a long walk from his shack.

Suddenly I realised that, given it was a twenty minute walk and he would probably fish there for an hour or so, and given that he would then take twenty minutes walking home, I had at least an hour and a half during which he would be away from the shack. It was perfect.

I veered back towards the bay and landed on the sandy strand not far from the captain's shack. I ran over the sand, then leapt over the boulders to the little shell-lined path. His door was unlocked. It always was. I opened it and ran across the room to the mantelpiece. There was the telescope. I hesitated only a moment before reaching for it. Then, tucking it under my arm, I hurried from the room and back down the path.

I raced away from the shack and ran up the nearest sand hill and skidded down the other side. I don't know why I was so determined to keep out of sight with the telescope. For all I knew old Captain Bass could have seen me wherever I was, would have known what I was up to however I tried to hide from him. It wouldn't really have surprised me if he'd deliberately gone fishing to give me the opportunity to filch the telescope and let it do its worst.

Because it could be its worst. I had a sudden vision of Jason lurching around the captain's living room training the telescope here and there, then stepping outside and . . . and then that silly Veronica doing exactly the same thing and . . . I saw them from time to time now, great fat rounded bodies like furry beanbags basking on the black rocks. If I took that risk would I be with them in the next few moments? Or would I be something worse? A squawking, bad-tempered red-beaked gull? A silver mullet – one of a thousand in a school? A bluebottle jellyfish? A bluebottle fly?

As these thoughts tumbled through my head I shrank from the telescope. All at once the risk of putting it to my eye seemed too much to think about: not such a smart idea. I laid it on the sand. When the captain had put it back on the mantelpiece he'd pushed it together. It now lay before me shining golden in the sun. All I needed to do was to reach out and draw it apart so that its four tubes were revealed – at which point it would be about half a metre long – then lift the narrowest tube with the eyepiece up to my eye.

I think what gave me pause was that although the captain had said this telescope showed you the future, not distance, as far as Jason and Veronica were concerned the future they were shown had not been at all distant. It was immediate, dramatic and horrible. One moment they were Jason or Veronica, the next they were large brown fur seals.

Just then, however, another shiny object caught my eye. It was something lodged in a clump of marram grass not far away. I stood up, curious, and wandered over. It was a pair of sunglasses, a pair with mirror lenses. The sunlight was reflecting off them. Then I remembered. These must have been the glasses Veronica was wearing when she'd been sunbathing that day. Bending down, I picked them up and studied them. As you do, I looked into the lenses. Nothing had changed: I still had no reflection. Nothing. It was a sickening feeling. I was a loblolly boy. The little mirrors couldn't see me. As far as reality was concerned, I did not exist.

That awful moment decided me. What did I have to lose? As a loblolly boy, I had no existence really; as a seal at least I could feel the world again: the sea, the sun, the taste of raw fish. I strode back to the telescope and seized it. I wrenched it apart and, without any further hesitation, swept it up to my eye.

I wasn't sure at first whether to feel relief or disappointment. At least there was no vision of a fat seal basking on a rock. But then, there wasn't a vision of anything. A couple of times when flying above the bay recently I had flown into low cloud. My first view through the telescope was rather like this. Grey, opalescent cloudiness. A swirling movement, but nothing hard, nothing sharp.

And then slowly, imperceptibly, the mist began to clear into a grey day. Shapes began to emerge. The sides of buildings. Windows. I could see wooden fences and a dark patch that seemed to be some sort of garden. Then I realised it *was* a garden, a vegetable garden with uneven rows of stunted cabbage plants and straggly beans. Then, strangely,

I was able to hear things: a flapping sound – the thwack of wet washing being hit by a cold wind. There was a long line of washing propped up by a tall pegged stick: grey sheets, shirts, and a row of knickers, like police exhibits. And then all at once I was aware of another movement. There was a figure there, bending, reaching up and pegging items to the line. It was a woman with a worn, weary face. Everything about her seemed grey: her hair, her face, her hands chapped and raw. I could not tell how old she was; she could have been anywhere between thirty and fifty. Curious, I trained the telescope on her and twisted the tube for focus. Surely I wasn't going to be reincarnated as a middle-aged woman hanging out knickers on a line?

Then the woman stretched up from her now empty basket and looked my way. I wondered momentarily whether she could actually see me standing in her backyard with a brass telescope trained on her. I needn't have worried. She was clearly directing her gaze at a figure behind me. Her expression was haggard and angry.

'Get that bloody dog out of here!' she shouted. 'If I've told you once, I've told you a thousand times – we don't want that bloody dog coming over here!'

I turned around and refocused. I could now see a weatherboard house and a crumbly concrete yard. A girl was sitting on a beer crate, a black labrador-cross at her feet. Through the grey I could now make out some colour. The girl was wearing a dark sweatshirt, but as I looked closely at her the darkness shifted to red, and I could see that her hair, which had been a nondescript dark colour, was also shifting to a rich red. I guessed she was pretty, but I couldn't really be sure. I hadn't had a lot to do with the girls at the Great House.

'Bella's not doing you any harm,' she yelled. 'She's a nice dog.'

'I don't care what kind of dog she is,' the voice yelled back. 'I don't want her coming over here and pooping all over our backyard. She's a dog, isn't she? All dogs are dirty!'

'Bella's not, are you, Bella darling,' said the red-haired girl, embracing the dog with both arms. The dog struggled to get as close to her as possible, licking with delight.

'I'm warning you, Suzy! If you don't get rid of that bloody dog, I'll knock you into the middle of next week!'

'Take no notice of her, Bella,' whispered Suzy. 'She's just a bad-tempered old cow.' All the same the girl stood up and twitched her backside angrily in the direction of the woman, who I guessed was her mother. 'Come on,' she said to the dog. 'We're getting out of here. I hate this stupid place anyway.' Then she disappeared around the side of the house, the black dog trotting happily and obediently behind. I glanced back at the mother, who was raising the clothes prop before gathering up the empty washing basket in her arms. She did not seem especially concerned that Suzy was leaving. Clearly her purpose had been to get rid of the dog.

I found I was more interested in the spiky young girl than her colourless mother, and so, telescope fixed, I followed her around the corner of the house. When the girl reached the corner, she gave a loud yell, which so alarmed the labrador that it leapt to one side. It alarmed me, too, and I nearly dropped the telescope.

'Meg!' she screamed. 'Meg! I'm going to the park with Bella! Wanna come?'

From inside the house came a muffled yell. 'Yeah, I do! Hang on a second!'

Moments later I could hear slamming doors and muffled running footsteps. Then the front door swung open and another girl, almost the double of Suzy, appeared on the front porch. Like Suzy, she had reddish hair and seemed quite pretty. Unlike Suzy she had a cheeky grin. I liked her immediately.

'Gunna be long?'

'Dunno. Come along, Bella!'

Clearly the two girls were sisters. Twin sisters. Clearly, too, in some way they were part of my future. It occurred to me that I might become one of them as Jason and Veronica had become seals. I wasn't sure that I liked that idea. I didn't know much about girls, as I've already explained. Of course, I might have been about to turn into the labrador. I didn't like that idea much either. I knew even less about labradors. I followed them as they made their way down the path to the road. Across the road was a line of weeping willow trees and a bank sloping to a murky-looking river. They turned right and headed off down the footpath. I was about to follow the little party when the mist came down and once again my view was swirling clouds of grey.

Some impulse made me keep the telescope to my eye. I was glad I did, for all at once the mist cleared. I was in a park. At first I thought I had arrived before the twins and Bella the dog, but when they didn't arrive and the park continued to be deserted I began to wonder what was going on. Not for long. Under some dark yew trees near the iron gates of the entrance, almost hidden in the shadows, I saw an unnatural-looking figure. At first I hadn't noticed him because he was dressed entirely in black. He was tall and bent, with narrow stovepipe trousers and a strange-looking black frock-coat. He looked like he'd stepped from some nineteenth-century storybook. The more I focused on him the more he reminded me of a picture of Abraham Lincoln I'd once seen. A silly-looking black beard followed the line of his chin like a woolly fringe, but he was otherwise clean-shaven. He had a long, pointed nose and was wearing wire-rimmed glasses with small round lenses.

I wondered what he was doing. Perhaps he was a lurker. One of those strange men in the park that mothers warn their children against. Then he drew from behind his back a long stick with a billowing net of gauze and he stepped, or rather pranced, into the light. Swinging the net expertly, he waltzed onto the lawn, following the path of a tiny object whose erratic movements in the air he was dancing a strange parody of on the ground. Then, with one last swinging swoop of the pole, he stopped and drew the net towards him. He laid it on the lawn and then hurried back to the bushes, returning with a glass jar. It seemed to have chopped-up leaves in it. I screwed the focus tightly and was able to see him draw from the net a delicate creature with triangular wings of iridescence: brilliant yellow with flashes of turquoise and orange. Quickly the butterfly was dropped into the jar and the lid screwed tightly. I saw a brief flutter as the wings opened and closed, then the wings closed forever.

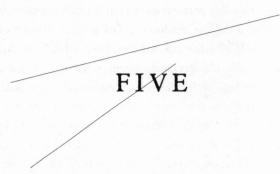

FIVE

AND THEN suddenly, briefly, there was swirling grey mist again. I say 'briefly' because all at once I found myself jerked into the air and I felt the telescope fall from my grip and drop to the ground. The bay and the sand dunes had all at once returned, but they were swinging about violently because I was moving about violently. I twisted around in alarm and found myself looking down into the face of Captain Bass.

'I see, loblolly boy,' he rasped angrily, 'you are on a quest as well, are you?'

'Put me down!' I shrieked.

He was so tall and his arms were so long that I seemed to be kicking my legs above his angry face.

'You are a very foolish little loblolly boy!' said the captain, ignoring my demand. 'Do you not realise how dangerous my telescope is? Didn't you see what happened to those other ignorant children?'

I felt myself getting angry then. 'I don't care what happened to them! I just needed to know what's going to happen to me. I'm sick of being this way. I want to be something real again.'

The captain let me down at last, gently enough, as it happened, and then he stooped and picked up the telescope, squeezed it together, and pushed it under his arm. 'Ah,' he said sadly. 'The difference between *wanting* and *getting*. Sometimes I think that difference is responsible for half the troubles of the world.'

'I don't care!' I said obstinately. 'I don't care! It's what I want.'

'It's not that easy,' sighed the old man. I didn't want to look at him. I knew he would have that faraway look in his ancient eyes, the look I was beginning to think was wisdom. I was suspicious of wisdom. I didn't think it would have the answer I wanted to hear.

'Do you really want to know what you must do?' asked Captain Bass, almost gently.

I stared at him. I didn't want to. I didn't really want to hear, because I knew there wouldn't be any easy answer.

'You will have to find someone to Exchange with,' said Captain Bass. 'Someone who can see you, and someone so desperate for change that they would be prepared to give up all the things of the world to be a loblolly boy. And that, as you well know,' he added, 'is a very big sacrifice. You'll have to be able to find someone prepared to give up their life for yours.'

I looked away. He was hateful. I hated him.

'I don't care,' I muttered.

'Ah, but you will,' he said. 'You see the trouble is, some-body like that is in such a dreadful situation that your life would be better than theirs. If you Exchange with them, you could well end up in a more terrible situation than you are in now.'

I looked at him once more. He was right, of course. But I hadn't really thought about it like that. I thought how I'd been so unhappy in the Great House, and then I thought how the boy who had been the loblolly boy now had to live that ghastly life. It seemed there was no way I could win.

I walked back across the beach with the old man to his shack. He didn't seem angry with me any more. That had passed quickly. He just seemed very sad, and that in many ways was worse.

When we got inside the little house, the captain went to a small cabinet and took out a bottle of dark navy rum. He added a large shot of this to a dirty tumbler of green-ginger wine, swirled the mixture round for a second or two then took a large swig. He screwed up his face and shook his head.

'It's horrible,' he said. 'Quite horrible.'

I noticed it didn't stop him taking another large swig, and then another.

Eventually, he put the tumbler down and glanced at me. 'Well, little loblolly boy,' he said, 'are you going to tell me what you saw through the telescope, or aren't you?'

'Who do you think they were?' I asked.

I'd finished telling the captain about the harrowed-looking woman and the twin girls. I'd told him too about the Abraham Lincoln look-alike with the butterfly net. The captain was in a much better mood than he had been before. I guessed that was because of the rum and green-ginger wine.

'I don't know. All I know is that you will see them some time in the future. That's what the telescope tells you. Whether you will become one of them or not, I have no idea. That may even be up to you . . .'

'Up to me?'

'Remember what I said. If they were Sensitives, you could arrange an Exchange with one of them, I suppose. That might be your decision . . .'

I thought about the two girls. I couldn't really see myself wanting to be either of them. For a start they were girls and I didn't know whether I'd like being a girl. And then the woman hanging out the washing was probably their mother. She'd been pretty grumpy. I couldn't see her being a lot of fun.

'What about the guy in the black suit?'

The captain looked thoughtful. 'Yes, I didn't like the sound of him. That was a laurel jar he had, you know . . .'

'A laurel jar?'

'Yes, insect collectors sometimes use them. They chop up fresh laurel leaves very finely and keep them in the jar. The leaves give off deadly fumes, so that when they put an insect in the jar it is killed. Quite effective, by the sound of it.'

Once again I recalled the man extricating the butterfly from the net. I saw its beautifully patterned wings flutter. I saw him unscrew the lid and drop the butterfly into the jar. I saw him close the lid. I saw the wings beat, twitch, and then stop moving altogether.

'A laurel jar,' I whispered.

The captain nodded.

However, I wasn't really thinking about the jar. I was thinking that the captain had used the word 'collector'. The man in the park with a butterfly net was a *Collector*.

I woke up next morning earlier than usual. It was just after dawn and the sun was still rising over the sea beyond the heads of the little bay. The sky was red, streaked with pink, grey and orange. The tall, dark figure of the captain stood before me.

I sat up, rubbing my eyes.

'What is it?'

'I've come to say goodbye, little loblolly boy.'

'Why, are you going somewhere?'

'No, little one. I'm not going anywhere. This is my home. You're going.'

'I am?'

He nodded. 'You must. You must go to the city. I heard your desperation yesterday. The telescope spoke to you. You must find your future . . .'

I looked around. The bay. The little houses. The odd wheeling gull.

'There are people in your future,' the captain said. 'And houses, streets. There are no people or houses or streets here.'

I climbed to my feet and shook myself. The captain was

71

right. There was no way I was going to get out of my crazy situation in this deserted little place. Not among the dunes, the seaweed and the driftwood, anyway. Perhaps I did need to find out what part Suzy and Meg and their mother were going to play in my future.

'So,' said the captain. 'I've come to say goodbye.'

I looked up at him. I guess he had been kind to me, although he'd often scared me, and he still scared me a little. He was unlike anybody I'd ever met. Now that he was standing before me saying goodbye I suddenly realised what he reminded me of. He was like a rock. One of those great black basalt rocks that rose out of the bay, withstanding anything the surging seas hurled at it. While I was here at the bay he would be here for me to cling to if I needed help. He would be my strength. Hard, of course. Rigid, sure. But utterly strong and able to resist anything. Once I left this place I would be completely on my own.

That realisation frightened me.

All the same, I knew with absolute certainty that I had to go, whatever dangers lay before me.

'Goodbye, Captain,' I said.

'I have something for you,' he said, digging into the pocket of his blue serge donkey jacket. He pulled out a small package wrapped in oilskin and tied with linen string. 'Don't open it now. It might come in handy . . .'

'Thank you,' I whispered.

'Well,' he said gruffly. 'Get on your way!'

Then he turned on his heels and strode off back towards his little cave house.

I slipped his gift inside my tunic, where it weighed heavily, and leapt into the air.

I felt the air's buoyancy immediately and found myself lifted higher and higher. Before the quickly diminishing figure of the captain had reached his door I was hundreds of metres above him. With a small pang of regret for the safety I was leaving behind me, I turned and stretched my body towards the north. Once again, I could see the hills of the peninsula give way to the plains as they stretched towards the mountains. I could see the line of the sea gird the coastline, leaving the roughly bitten bays and inlets of the hilly coast and then following the line of the plains in a long, smooth beach that curved in a great arc northwards.

Beyond lay the city, shrouded in a brown-and-grey gauze of smog barely penetrated by the early-morning sun. Somewhere in its hidden depths lay the tall walls and grey stone buttresses of the Great House – the Great House I was now free of. Hidden in its depths, too, was the backyard I had seen in the captain's telescope: the struggling vegetable garden, the crumbling concrete, the teetering clothes prop and, I guessed, the weary-looking woman and her twin daughters.

I tried to remember what I had seen. The place, as I recalled it, was nondescript. But then I remembered there had been a river across the road. And weeping willow trees.

I swooped down and down until I was low enough for the smog to dissipate. I looked right and left for the telltale silver tail of a river. Of course, as I looked about me, there were several rivers. The two largest twisted like shiny serpents through the tree-filled suburbs. It didn't take me long to realise that what I was trying to do was useless. I had only the vaguest notion of what the house looked like, let alone what street it was on or what river the street bordered. It was needle and haystack. I had almost given way to a welling disappointment when I remembered what the captain had said. The telescope brought the future closer; the things I had seen through its lens were part of my future. There was no need to actively seek them. They would find me, sooner or later.

Feeling less agitated, I dropped through the air and landed at random on what turned out to be a busy street corner. Having lived for so long in the Great House, I had rarely seen trucks, cars or motorbikes. Now, as they whooshed past me on all sides, I shrank into myself beside the window of a corner shop, a little frightened by their speed and noise. Quite a number of people came and went, walking purposefully along the footpath, and every so often one would brush past me and enter the shop to buy a paper or a piece of fruit. No one, as far as I could tell, was remotely aware of my existence. One woman even stood in front of me for a few moments as she checked her reflection in the shop window. She dabbed at her cheek and frowned a little and was obviously looking right through me. It was weird. Once she had gone, I turned around. There was no reflection of me in the window, just the darkened colours of passing traffic.

This was too much, especially after the solitude of the little bay. I needed to get to somewhere quiet, peaceful. I set off down the street and within a block I found the entrance to a school. It was still early as I hurried through the gates and out into the playground. There was a line of tall elm trees where the asphalt ended and the sports fields began, and underneath them was a row of benches. Gratefully, I sat down to gather myself and plan what to do next.

There were a few kids about. A small group was kicking a soccer ball about the field and others were standing about in twos and threes. Idly, I scanned them to see if any of the girls had red hair, but I couldn't see anybody who looked like Suzy or Meg.

I became aware of the package tucked in my tunic. It was heavy and awkward. Curious, I pulled it out. Captain Bass had tied the string into fiendish nautical knots. I didn't have a knife, of course. I felt the package, but that didn't give me many clues. It was clumpy, shapeless and heavy. It could have been anything.

Reasoning that I didn't have anything better to do, I began patiently picking at the knots. It took ages. Gradually, however, I was able to work a loop in one of the knots and very gradually I was able to work another. Finally, I was able to draw the knot-ends through the loops and that allowed me to work more loops and slowly, surely, all the knots began to unravel.

I wound the string into a small ball. All that remained to do was to unwrap the oilskin cloth and the captain's gift would be revealed. And there it was: a small model train engine. It was beautiful. It was perfect. The small, flanged wheels had been skilfully engineered, and the chimney was so real I could almost imagine it puffing smoke. The engine was finished in gunmetal-black and racing-green paint with brass trims. Beside the cylinder box was lettered the number 14701. The cab, too, was so beautifully finished I could almost imagine a couple of tiny firemen shovelling coal into the firebox. There were, of course, no little men, but there was something else I noticed in the cab.

It was a small piece of folded paper.

I drew it out and unfolded it. Somebody, I guessed the captain, had written in tiny but very neat capital letters: TO BE RETURNED.

I held the engine before me for some time in quiet admiration, then I wrapped it up carefully once more in the oilskin cloth, and squeezed it back into my pocket. It was a most curious gift. Why on earth had Captain Bass given me a tiny model engine? I'd never expressed any interest in model trains. I didn't really care about them. The engine was a beautiful work of art, but it wasn't something I could see being of any use to me in my present existence. It didn't make any sense at all. It was the oddest gift I'd ever received.

But then I thought about the scrap of paper. It seemed it wasn't even a gift. TO BE RETURNED. It was apparently only a loan. I was quite confused. It seemed that the captain thought I'd be delighted to lug around this heavy object until I found the time or the opportunity to get it back to him. Why? I had no idea how long whatever I was about to do would take. I hadn't even any idea *what* I was about to do, except somehow meet up with the twins I'd seen through the telescope. When this would happen, where this would happen, even *whether* this would happen was still a mystery.

And now, while I was waiting, I had to carry a locomotive in my tunic. It was stupid.

I'd been so absorbed in untying the parcel and then trying to make sense of the model train that I'd been completely unaware of the playground filling up with children. They were now all about me. Big ones, little ones, quiet ones and noisy, bouncy ones. Shouting, running, kicking, skipping and throwing things. I felt as though I were in the centre of a tremendous field of energy. It would almost have been enjoyable but for the sickening knowledge that not one of the children could see me. Not one was aware of my presence. I was a ghost. Invisible.

For all that, it was chaotic and colourful. Until the sudden, loud ringing of a staticky bell broadcast over a public address system. Immediately, obediently, all the children rushed off towards the classrooms and formed themselves into messy lines. Teachers emerged to wait on the wooden verandahs until the messy lines became slightly less messy, and then each, with a wagging finger, signalled the line to climb the steps and enter the classroom.

Within minutes the playground and the sports field were deserted and silent once more. In a way, though, nothing had changed. I was just as alone in the empty playground as I had been in the crowded one. I stood up, feeling very depressed. I was alone and bored. I had nothing to do, nowhere to go, nobody to talk to. And what made it all the more depressing was that this great nothingness could well be the rest of my life.

I tried as best I could to shrug off the feeling and jumped into the air once more. Perhaps things might look a little better from a higher perspective, I thought. There was a flagpole erected before the oldest building, probably the original school. I flew up to it and perched on top like an oversized green pigeon. It wasn't particularly comfortable but it did give me a great view of the school and the surrounding neighbourhood. I hadn't been up there for very long before I heard an excited barking from down below. It was coming from somewhere in the schoolyard but a building was in the way.

Then a skinny black labrador ran around a corner and into view. It was shortly pursued by a small figure.

'Bella!' shouted the figure. 'Bella! Go home!'

Bella clearly had no intention of going home. Bella was far more interested in playing a wild game of chase-me across the soccer field. A second figure came into view. She too was shouting, 'Bella! Bella!'

I immediately recognised the two red-haired girls I'd seen through the telescope.

Before they reached the playing field in pursuit of the dog, another shout rent the air. A teacher had run out of a classroom and was bellowing from the verandah: 'Suzy! Meg! Come into the classroom immediately!'

'Sorry, Miss,' cried Meg over her shoulder, with a beaming grin. 'Sorry, Miss. We have to catch Bella!'

The teacher somehow managed to turn the volume up even further. '*Meg!* You have to do no such thing! Leave that dog alone instantly and get into the *classroom!*'

The command was so forceful, an ordinary army would have obeyed it without question. But not Meg. She gave her teacher another grin and a cheery wave and carried on after the dog.

Suzy hadn't even bothered responding to the teacher. Apart from a quick contemptuous glance over her shoulder, she'd ignored her totally and had pulled well ahead of Meg in the chase after the dog.

Bella, meanwhile, was bouncing joyously over the playing fields towards the soccer goal, the girls in hot pursuit. All at once, my sad mood lifted. I wanted to be part of the fun. I stood up on the cap of the flagpole then leapt into the air. My wings stretched out and allowed me to glide gracefully down. I landed a few metres behind the girls. Bella, who, I began to realise, would not have won any prizes either for canine obedience or for canine intelligence, had managed to trap herself in a soccer goal that had a net attached. Suzy was advancing from the right, and Meg was advancing from the left. Bella was woofing happily, running back and forth like a first-division goalkeeper. The teacher was still standing on the verandah with her arms on her hips, looking just like a furious teapot.

I was able to see the problem right away. Suzy and Meg had trapped Bella fairly and squarely, but they had no way of securing her. All they would be able to do would be to hold her by the collar and walk her home. From the expression on their teacher's face, though, I didn't think that idea was much of a goer.

It didn't take Suzy and Meg long to realise the problem either. With a stern 'Bella!' Suzy grabbed the dog by its scruff and then stood there, staring helplessly at her sister.

'What do we do now?' she asked.

Instinctively, they both turned about as if seeking help. By this time, I was right behind them. To my amazement, Meg said, 'Hello. You wouldn't have anything we could tie Bella up with, would you?'

I spun around to see who she could have been talking to. There was nobody there. I turned back to her, astonished.

'You can *see* me?' She would be the only person who'd been able to see me with the exception of Captain Bass and a seagull.

Meg gave her sister a sideways glance. 'Of course I can see you! Why shouldn't I be able to see you? I'm not blind, am I?'

I was thrown for a second. 'Well,' I stammered, 'not everybody can see me . . .'

'Don't be so stupid,' Suzy snapped. 'Just tell us. Do you or don't you have anything we can tie this silly dog up with? Cos if you don't, maybe you could run away and get us something!'

Suzy could see me too!

I was about to shake my head when I remembered the string that had been wrapped about the captain's parcel. 'Well, I do, actually,' I mumbled, and handed her the little ball. 'I don't know whether it's long enough, though.'

Meg grabbed it, giving me a quick, grateful smile. She shook it out into loops and passed one end to Suzy, who grunted 'thanks' and tied one end to Bella's collar. She unravelled the rest of the string and tied the other end to a goal post. 'That should fix her.'

'She can stay there till playtime, anyway. We can take her back to Mrs Osborne then,' said Meg.

'Yeah. We'd better get into class. Look at her. Old Ma Tasker's going spare. What a stupid old cow.' Suzy stared belligerently towards their teacher. 'One of these days . . .' she said.

Meg giggled nervously. 'Look at her! We'd better hurry . . .'

'Don't you dare,' said Suzy. 'It only encourages her. Take your time . . .' Then she looked at me curiously. 'Thanks,' she said. 'I haven't seen you about before. Whose class are you in?'

'I don't go to this school,' I said.

Both girls were staring at me.

'What school do you go to then?' asked Meg.

That was a problem. There had been a school at the Great House, but I didn't go there any more. The thing I had become didn't go to school at all. That seemed to me to be the safest answer.

'I don't,' I said.

The girls looked at me with new respect. 'You don't?' asked Suzy.

I shook my head.

'Hey, where'd you get those clothes?' asked Meg. 'They're wild.'

I shrugged. 'I don't know. They sort of came with me . . .'

I knew it sounded crazy as soon as I said it. Once again the girls exchanged glances.

'You're weird!' exclaimed Suzy. But she laughed.

I had to admit I liked these girls, even Suzy. They seemed somehow to be free spirits. I guessed I must look strange and I guessed I was saying very strange things, but it didn't seem to faze them one little bit. I laughed too. Not just because I'd met these oddball twins, but because I was no longer alone. I'd found people to talk to. I found myself grinning too.

'Hey, Suzy,' said Meg, glancing towards the verandah. 'If we don't get back to the classroom Old Tasker's going to explode. Look at her.'

The teacher was still standing there gesticulating wildly.

Suzy giggled. 'Yeah, and there'll be blood and bones and bits of flesh stuck all over the walls of the classrooms. And we'll get the blame!'

'As usual,' laughed Meg. 'Look,' she said to me. 'Thanks for the string and stuff. And could you do us a terrific favour? Could you find a bucket of water or something and bring it over for Bella? I don't want to leave her out here for all that time without . . .'

I nodded. 'No problem,' I said. 'See you later.'

'Bye!' shouted the girls. And together they rushed off towards the classroom, almost as quickly as they'd raced away from it in pursuit of the dog.

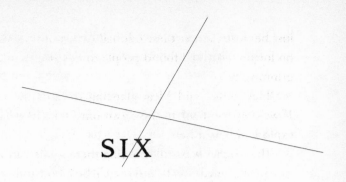

SIX

GETTING A bucket of water for Bella wasn't that easy. I mean, how many buckets do you normally find lying about a school playground? I wandered about the place for a while but the only things I could find that you could keep water in were a plastic bag or two and a large pottle that had once held popcorn.

It was a little strange going past the classrooms where all the kids were getting their morning dose of teacher. You'd think it would have made me grateful to be free of all that stuff, but in actual fact it made me sadder and sadder. I felt excluded. I couldn't even go into one of the classrooms and say, *Hey, hey, let me do some sums*, or, *Got any spelling for me?* I knew if I'd done so, nobody would have taken a blind bit of notice. Someone may have seen the door open and the wind brush the curtain, but somebody else would have gone over and closed the door. Nobody would have seen me. Nobody would have heard me.

I could, I guess, have gone into the room with the twins and their teacher, Old Ma Tasker; but if the twins had said anything to me, the others in the class would have thought they were crazy. Had flipped.

Finally I was forced to spread my wings and fly off in search of something. I put the engine down beside the goal post, hoping nobody would find it. Beyond the school I was quickly able to locate the river I had seen in the telescope. It was lined with weeping willow trees and its banks were gently sloping lawns. At least I knew where I could get water. Not long after, in the grounds of a newly-built house, I saw an empty plastic paint bucket that the painters had left behind. I flew down and grabbed it, then returned to the river. After filling the bucket in a swooping dive, I rose once more into the air and glided back to the school.

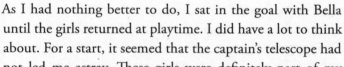

As I had nothing better to do, I sat in the goal with Bella until the girls returned at playtime. I did have a lot to think about. For a start, it seemed that the captain's telescope had not led me astray. These girls were definitely part of my future. Right now, in fact, they were part of my present.

The second and perhaps more exciting point was that they could *see* me. They were – how had the captain described them? – Sensitives. As I had been. I had understood that Sensitives were very few and far between, and yet all at once I had discovered two. Things were looking up. Surely one of these girls could be persuaded to Exchange with me. The woman who was their mother looked to be a pretty grumpy creature. Either Meg or Suzy might be really pleased to be released from her and instead lead a life of freedom: to be able to fly and be invisible.

However, as I waited with Bella, who had accepted her reality and settled into a patient sleep, I was able to consider the situation more carefully. The first thing I thought about was the reality of the Exchange. Sure, Suzy or Meg could become the loblolly boy that I had become, or in their case, perhaps, loblolly girl. And there lay the problem. I would then be Exchanged into the body of a girl. I would have to be Suzy or Meg. And that would mean I would have to live with the grumpy woman, be in the class with that crosspatch school teacher. Was this what I really wanted?

What *did* I want?

I wanted to be me again. I wanted to be myself, the boy I had been in the Great House.

Becoming Suzy or Meg would just be another frying pan/fire situation. It didn't seem fair. It didn't seem fair at all.

I guess I must have dozed off because I was suddenly aroused by the jarring sound of the school bell ringing once more. I looked about and children were streaming out of the classrooms and hurrying towards the playing fields. It was playtime at last.

Sure enough, only a few minutes later I could distinguish the running figures of the twins coming towards me. Bella saw them too, and began to bark enthusiastically. Her barking attracted a crowd of kids, drawn by the novelty of a friendly dog tied up in the soccer goal. Suzy and Meg had to push through them to get to the dog and me.

'Thanks,' gasped Suzy. 'Thanks for taking care of her.'

I gave her a small smile. One or two of the kids had given Suzy a strange look because, to them, she must have appeared to have been talking to herself, and I didn't want to embarrass her by encouraging any more talk. Instead I put my fingers to my lips. She was a smart cookie. She looked around and immediately seemed to realise that none of her friends had any idea of my presence. Her eyes widened momentarily at the knowledge, and then she gave me a small secret grin. A warning glance to Meg was all it took, and Meg seemed to be in the know as well.

'Come on, Bella,' she said, untying the string from the goal post. 'We're going to take you home to Mrs Osborne. If the dog ranger catches you, he'll take you to the pound.'

'Suzy, you can't do that,' said one of the other kids. 'Old Ma Tasker will go spare if you leave the grounds.'

'You know what happened last time,' said another.

'I don't care,' said Suzy. 'She's got no feeling for dogs. Bella can't stay here all day, tied up. She'll die of boredom.'

'We'll have to take her home,' said Meg.

'Anyway,' added Suzy. 'Who cares about stupid Old Ma Tasker?'

'I do!' said a loud and very stern voice.

Everybody turned at once. I did as well. There standing at the edge of the press of kids was Old Ma Tasker herself. I guess she'd been attracted by the crowd, but she must have moved quickly and silently. I certainly hadn't noticed her.

I was fascinated by the reaction of the kids. Nobody wanted to be close to the source of the trouble, but everybody wanted to see what would happen. Accordingly, like melting butter, the crowd slipped away, but not too far. It coalesced again about four or five metres behind the teacher. Within seconds the only ones near the goal posts were Meg, Suzy, Bella and me. But, of course, I didn't count.

'I understand, girls,' said the teacher severely, 'that you were planning to leave the school grounds in the company of that particularly scruffy-looking hound?'

'It's not a hound, Mrs Tasker,' said Meg. 'It's a labrador.'

'I don't care, Meg, if it's a Kodiak bear,' said Mrs Tasker acidly. 'You are not going anywhere – with that dog or without it.'

'You can't stop us!' said Suzy. Defiantly perhaps, but also bravely, I thought. Old Ma Tasker wasn't as impressed. She obviously thought Suzy was simply being cheeky.

'I certainly *can*!' she said ferociously. So ferociously that even Bella whimpered and crouched down again, as close to the ground as she could get, her ears flat against the top of her head.

Meg and Suzy, brave as they were, kind of crumpled. Obviously you didn't mess very far with Old Ma Tasker. It was sad to see the spirit knocked out of them just like that. I felt sorry for them. So sorry, I felt an overwhelming urge to help them. But how? I was invisible to Old Ma Tasker. I may as well not have been there.

'Go to my room, the pair of you!' said Old Ma Tasker as fiercely as before. 'We will discuss this matter, but we will not discuss it before an audience!'

The other children were looking somewhat wilted. The twins looked around desperately. Everybody avoided their eyes.

'Off you go!' Mrs Tasker commanded.

The twins were truly beaten. Heads bowed, they set off forlornly for the classroom.

'You others,' snapped Mrs Tasker, scanning the shrinking crowd for any dissent. 'Go away and play. I do not like unruly mobs!'

Suzy and Meg were now several metres on their way. The other children, the bravest grinning self-consciously, scattered lest Old Ma Tasker should point her angry finger their way. When she was satisfied she was being obeyed, Mrs Tasker turned and hurried after the girls.

I glanced around. It was upsetting to see the girls so humiliated. Once again I felt that overwhelming urge to do something about it.

And then I saw the bucket of water. It was still sitting in the goal-mouth next to Bella. She had only had a couple of gulping mouthfuls. Suddenly, I knew what I must do. I seized the handle and leapt into the air. I soared higher and higher and then, when I was directly above the teacher, I dived down again holding the bucket of water carefully in my outstretched hand, so as not to spill a drop. I needed every one. God knows what any kids thought who saw a bucket flying unaided through the air. If any had glanced that way, they must have been struck dumb with silent wonder, for absolutely nothing was said.

When I was only a metre or two above the striding teacher, I upended the bucket. The whole bucketful landed on her frizzled head and splashed all over her, drenching her in an instant. She gave a sudden gasping squawk of surprise and turned around to see who had committed such an outrage. There was nobody there; all the children had long

88

since scattered. She spun back to look at the girls, but they were still several metres in front of her. Besides, she'd had them in her sights the whole time.

She looked up towards me. Water was still streaming down her face, and her sopping clothes clung to her shapeless body. Her hair was bedraggled and sticking to her head, and rivulets had streaked down her powdered face, striping it as they did so.

'Who did this?' she wailed to nobody in particular.

And then she gasped as she saw the now empty bucket still hovering several metres above her. To the distressed woman it must have seemed as though the bucket were hanging on a sky-hook.

The twins had turned around at the sudden commotion and were now staring in amazement at the sight of the drenched teacher. Then they followed her astonished gaze and saw me.

Not only could the girls see me, they could see me in flight. My great green wings were stretched out and flexing. I must have seemed like an angel the colour of avocado.

'Wow,' Suzy breathed in wonder.

'Hey!' sighed Meg.

'No! No! No!' cried Old Ma Tasker blindly and, dripping water and leaving great puddling footsteps on the asphalt, she rushed past the girls to the safety of her classroom.

———————

As the bedraggled teacher scurried away I wafted down to land, gently moving my wings back and forth. The girls were transfixed in wonder.

'What *are* you?' asked Suzy. The words were uttered even before my feet had touched the ground. I flung the bucket to one side.

'Have you come from space?' asked Meg. 'Are you an alien?'

The question rocked me a little. I had simply accepted what I had become. It had never occurred to me that I might be an alien. I simply knew that I had become a loblolly boy. What a loblolly boy *was* hadn't really troubled me before.

'From Mars?' added Meg. Her tone was rather hopeful. I had the impression she'd be disappointed if I wasn't.

I shook my head. 'I'm a loblolly boy,' I said.

'A *what*?' asked Suzy.

'Are those wings real?' asked Meg.

'Of course they're real,' I said.

'What's a loblolly boy?' demanded Suzy.

I didn't really know how to answer her. 'Me,' I said. 'I'm a loblolly boy . . .'

'You're not answering the question!' Suzy said.

'Can you really fly?' whispered Meg.

'Of course he can really fly, you dweeb!' snapped Suzy. 'You saw him. Nice work with the bucket,' she said to me, a little begrudgingly.

'I thought you could do with some help,' I said.

'If you're not from space . . .' began Meg.

'How did you do that?' demanded Suzy.

I shrugged. 'I don't know. How do you ride a bike? I just spread my wings and leap into the air . . .'

'Oh, great,' said Suzy sarcastically. 'He just spreads his

wings and leaps into the air. Easy-peasy. Did it occur to you that most people don't have wings?'

I shrugged again. I remembered how I'd thought *my* loblolly boy had seemed so frustratingly stupid to me, as I must seem stupid to these girls. All the same, how on earth could I possibly explain? 'They don't, but I do,' I said simply.

'Yes, I know. I saw them. But *how* did you get them?'

It was all getting very complicated. 'I Exchanged,' I said.

'Exchanged?'

'I came across a loblolly boy and we Exchanged,' I said.

'I don't understand any of this,' said Meg.

'Neither do I,' said Suzy. 'What do you mean?'

I shrugged again. I didn't even understand it myself. 'It's sort of hard to explain,' I said. 'I met this loblolly boy in the garden, and he said he could teach me how to fly. I thought it was some kind of silly game and went along with it. Nothing happened, of course. I spent some time jumping up and down like a stupid yoyo. I thought he was just joking. Then he called the guards and the dogs came running and I felt really frightened. The loblolly boy grabbed my hand and told me to jump, so I jumped and jumped, and there was a flash and suddenly I was flying. But what had happened was that we had Exchanged – he had become me and I had become him . . .'

'Wow,' sighed Meg.

Suzy was staring at me doubtfully. 'You became him . . .' she said.

I nodded.

'That's the craziest thing I've ever heard.'

I nodded again. 'I know. I know. If you think it's crazy, how do you think I feel about it?'

Just then, Bella began to bark. Meg turned towards her. 'Suzy,' she said. 'Let's take Bella home. I don't think Old Tasker's going to worry about what we do now.'

Suzy was still looking at me curiously. Then she turned to her sister. 'Why not?' she said. 'You want to come too?' she asked me.

'No problem,' I said.

For the first time, she gave me a little grin.

'Good,' she said. 'Let's go.'

I felt suddenly much lighter. I leapt into the air once more and glided back to the soccer goal. The parcel was still there and I was able to gather it into my arms before the girls arrived to retrieve Bella. She woofed happily as they untethered her and then we set off together, across the field, across the asphalt, past the classroom, and out the school gates.

'How come we can see you and nobody else can?' demanded Suzy. 'I mean none of the other kids could see you, could they?'

'Old Ma Tasker couldn't either,' added Meg.

We were sitting in the twins' living room. It wasn't much of a room. The carpet was old and threadbare and had the sort of awful swirling pattern on it that would have made you feel seasick if it had been new – now it just looked as though lots of people had been seasick all over it. The paint was peeling in places and the furniture looked as if it had been bought when the charity shop was having a sale. The girls didn't seem to notice though.

'Well,' demanded Suzy, like a dog worrying a bone. 'How come none of the other kids can see you?'

'Where're your mum and dad?' I asked. I didn't know that I wanted to answer Suzy's question. If I did, I'd have to explain that they were Sensitives, and that they had the ability to Exchange with me. I didn't want them to know that yet.

'Mum's at work,' said Meg. 'And Dad doesn't live here any more.'

'He took off with Michael,' said Suzy bitterly, and then added: 'And his new girlfriend. She was a real mole.'

'Do you want a crisp?' asked Meg. She passed the brightly coloured foil bag to me.

I shook my head. 'I don't eat any more,' I said.

Meg looked at me sadly. Suzy looked at me with astonishment. 'What a bummer!' she said. 'I couldn't cope with that.'

I nodded. 'Yeah, it is. I miss it. I'd love to taste a crisp again . . . But who's Michael?'

'Our dorky brother,' said Suzy casually, with a toss of her hair.

'How can you say that, Suzy?' protested Meg. 'We never even met him. He was gone before we were old enough to know him,' she said to me.

'Well he must have been dorky to have gone with *him*,' said Suzy flatly.

Suzy lapsed into silence, and Meg nibbled sadly at her

crisps. I felt that, of the two of them, I liked Meg far more. She was gentler and not so bitter. Suzy was up and down, quite unpredictable. I didn't know where I was with her.

Now Suzy turned on me again. 'Anyway, you never answered our question.'

'What question?'

'How come we can see you and nobody else can?'

I shrugged. 'I don't know. You must have special powers of sight, I guess.'

Suzy laughed. 'You have special powers of flight. We have special powers of sight! I'm a poet. I know what I'd prefer though . . . Can we see your wings?'

I shook my head. 'Uh uh. Better not. They're pretty fragile . . .'

That was a white lie. As a matter of fact I had no idea how fragile my wings were. But I'd been noticing the way Suzy was looking at me. I felt she was getting far too interested in what it might take to learn to fly.

SEVEN

'MEG?' I asked. 'Would you do me a favour?'

We were sitting in the girls' backyard. It was exactly as I'd seen it through the telescope. A scruffy vegetable garden gone to seed and weeds. A lawn, badly in need of a mow, a crumbling concrete square and, down the back, a sagging clothesline.

Meg looked at me curiously. 'Depends what it is,' she said. Her tone wasn't suspicious though, as I guessed Suzy's would have been.

We were on our own. The girls had made themselves a lunch of another bag of salt-and-vinegar crisps, then Suzy had taken Bella home to the neighbours.

'Would you look after this for me? I'm sick of lugging it about.' I handed her the parcel the captain had entrusted me with.

'Sure,' said Meg, glancing at it with some interest. 'What is it? Is it precious?'

'I don't really know. Maybe. You can look at it if you like. It's not a secret or anything.'

Meg unwrapped the oilskin carefully. 'It's a model train!'

I nodded.

'Whose is it? Yours?'

'Sort of. There's this guy called Captain Bass. He gave it to me.'

'That's a crazy kind of present,' said Meg.

'Yes. But what's even crazier is that he gave it to me, and then he told me I had to return it.'

'What sort of a present is that?'

'I know. Doesn't really make sense, does it? You have somewhere safe?'

Meg gave me a meaningful glance. She may have been the gentler twin, but she was just as sharp as her sister. She knew what I meant: *somewhere safe from Suzy.* She nodded. 'I'm sure I can find somewhere,' she said.

Not long after that, Suzy came back. She was immediately restless. She flopped about like a fish on the sand.

'God, I hate this dump,' she said, glancing about the backyard. 'I wish I could just get away.'

'We could go for a walk or something,' suggested Meg.

'That wasn't what I meant,' said Suzy.

It had occurred to me that they should really have been getting back to school, but somehow I didn't think it was worth mentioning. I wondered what Suzy did mean. She sounded quite unhappy.

'We could go to the park,' said Meg. 'You know, we could show him our secret place . . .'

She glanced at me, then back at her sister. Suzy nodded.

'Okay,' she said. 'Beats hanging around here, I suppose.'

I was aware that when Meg had called me 'him' it was because she didn't have a name for me. I realised that I didn't have a name for myself. I used to have a name, but now it belonged to the one who had been the loblolly boy. I felt a pang of sadness. My name had disappeared along with my appetite and my visibility. It was just another reminder of how I had become a non-person.

✕

The park wasn't too far away. I recognised it as soon as we got near. It was the park I had seen through the captain's telescope. There were the iron railings painted green, the wrought-iron gates with the spikes on top, and the dusty black yew trees guarding the entrance.

It was all but deserted, which wasn't surprising; at this time of the early afternoon kids were at school and grown-ups at work. We walked down the asphalt paths past the formal rose garden with the broken bird bath.

'Where is this place?' I asked, curious.

'Not far,' said Suzy.

She was right. It was only a few more metres along the main path.

'Here we are . . .'

Where we were was another path that led off on a diagonal and into a grove of very old linden trees. They were tall and their lower branches dangled to the ground like ancient ballerinas' arms. Underneath, the branches formed a leafy canopy like a great green tent, until you broke through on the other side to an inner circular lawn. In the middle of the lawn was a small octagonal building with walls of white trellis and a roof like an oriental hat.

'Hey!' I whispered.

'It's a gazebo,' said Suzy proudly.

'A ga-what?'

'A gazebo. Like an old-fashioned summerhouse.'

'Oh.'

'Don't you know anything?' she asked sarcastically.

'I know how to fly!'

That shut her up for a few moments.

'Hardly anybody knows it's here,' said Meg. 'It's surrounded by those great big trees.'

'What do you do here?' I asked.

'Nothing special,' said Suzy. 'It's just our own private place.'

'It's our own little world,' added Meg.

There was a step up into the gazebo and we entered. It wasn't very big. Inside it wasn't really much bigger than the top of a dinner table. There was a bench all around the outer wall and we sat down. The light dappled through the criss-cross of the trellis. I had to admit it was a pretty cool place.

Just then, a sudden movement caught my eye and I glanced back out through the entrance.

'Somebody else knows it's here,' I murmured. 'It's not so private right now . . .'

The girls followed my gaze.

'Oh, bloody hell,' muttered Suzy. 'It's that crazy guy again. What does he want to come here for and spoil everything?'

I felt a momentary chill. There prancing round the lawn, just as I'd seen him through the telescope, was the strange, tall, gaunt Abraham Lincoln-like figure, wearing the same skinny black trousers and the same weird black frock-coat. Just as he had that first time, he was carrying the butterfly net and swinging it occasionally at some unseen target. If the telescope had really given a glimpse into my future, then this weird figure was going to feature somehow.

'Do you know him?' I whispered. 'Who is he?'

'We don't really know,' whispered Meg. 'He lives in an old two-storey house on Sylvan Street. We went past it on the way here. It's got a great big laurel hedge in front of it so you can hardly see it.'

'I wish I could hardly see him,' said Suzy. 'He gives me the creeps.'

'He's always chasing butterflies and moths and flying insects,' said Meg.

'Yeah,' said Suzy. 'He should pick on somebody his own size.'

'He's an entomologist, I suppose,' said Meg.

'What's that?' I asked.

'A gold-plated weirdo,' said Suzy flatly.

As if he'd heard her, the entomologist or whatever he was stopped his prancing and looked towards the gazebo. We ducked down, but too late. He'd seen the girls and came wandering over in his strange, loping strides.

'Hello!' he called. 'Didn't see you there!'

He came right up and peered inside the little octagonal room. Up close he looked even stranger, with his funny round glasses with the heavy, pebble lenses. He seemed to start with surprise at the sight of the girls and took off the glasses and rubbed at them vigorously. Then he put them on again with a small grunt of satisfaction and looked about the gazebo once more. He grinned at the girls. He had bad teeth. 'Look!' he said. He was holding up a jar. Inside the jar was a dead butterfly. It was small and golden-red, with iridescent turquoise edges on its lifeless wings.

'Ugh!' said Meg instinctively.

'Did you kill that?' asked Suzy.

'It's a Matheson Gold,' said the entomologist. 'Quite rare. I've only got a couple of other specimens.'

'Did you kill it?' repeated Suzy.

'Quite painless,' said the entomologist. 'I use a laurel bottle, you know.'

'That's horrible!' said Suzy.

'Do you think so?' asked the entomologist, surprised. 'Personally, I think it's quite beautiful.'

His voice was thin and rather high-pitched, as if it had been filtered through small sharp stones. Again, he looked around the gazebo curiously. It seemed he was looking for something that wasn't there. I hoped it wasn't me. It was unlikely. He gave no indication whatever of having seen me. All the same, something about him gave me the creeps, so I kept perfectly still.

'Not at school today?' he asked.

'We're sick,' said Meg hurriedly.

'Sick?' asked the entomologist. 'You don't look sick to me. What's wrong with you?'

'We're sick of dead butterflies,' said Suzy.

That was a pretty cheeky thing to say, but I have to say I admired her for it. 'Come on, Meg,' she said. 'Let's get out of here. I don't like this place any more.'

She gave the man a scornful look and pushed past him, Meg following. He stepped hurriedly aside as they swept past. For some reason I stayed where I was. I still had the strange feeling that I shouldn't move lest the very air should give me away. More and more I was getting a bad feeling from this man. I wondered why the captain's telescope had made such a point of letting me see him as he pranced and danced around the park, swiping at butterflies.

The man gave the gazebo another curious once-over, but again apparently without seeing me, and then he returned to the lawn. Suzy and Meg by this time had reached the circle of linden trees and pushed their way hurriedly through them.

I let them go. I didn't want to leave what I imagined was the safety of the gazebo. All the while I kept the entomologist in sight. He didn't seem to want to go either. He seemed to stay for hours. For long periods he'd stay still, rather like a cat: motionless, waiting. Then, presumably catching a flicker of wings or something, he'd leap and swish at the air with his long-handled net.

I longed to be able to step out onto the lawn myself, and leap into the air and fly up and over the linden trees and out of the park. To swing and swoop through the sky with perfect poise, to hover on an updraft – my wings outstretched and perfectly still, as if cupped in the very hands of the air. Or, for a thrill, to beat my wings into a blur and soar upwards before plunging again in a steep trajectory, my hair, my silky clothes streaming behind. I wanted to climb through the gossamer clouds, until their blankets hid the park, the streets, the suburb, the city itself . . . so high I'd be surrounded only by white and blue, the sky above me, clouds below me, the scalloped sea far in the distance.

Yet some tiny little voice inside me told me that this would not be a good idea, that I should stay stock still and never let that strange black figure out of sight.

And then, finally, as suddenly as he'd appeared, he disappeared.

I almost missed his leaving. He'd danced across the lawn in pursuit of some tiny creature and then all at once he'd bounded under the canopy of the linden trees and out of sight. I waited, half expecting him to prance back again as mysteriously as he'd departed, but the minutes ticked by and there was no re-emergence. At last, I was persuaded that the entomologist had really given up and gone.

Gingerly, I didn't know why, I stepped from the gazebo and stared up at the circle of sky surrounded by the heart-shaped foliage of the linden trees. Everything was silent apart from the rustling whisper of the wind in the leaves. I lifted my arms and my wings unfolded, then gratefully I leapt up and, catching the faintest breath of a breeze, I soared higher, higher, until I was as high in the air as the treetops, and then higher, higher until they were merely circles of green below me.

From that great height I looked below to find my bearings. The park was a great square of green dotted with trees and gardens divided by the black rectangular lines of the asphalt paths. Surrounding the park were the gridlines of the streets, lined with houses stranded beside their drives and marooned between their front yards and their backyards.

I was really more interested in the streets and where the twins were and, to be honest, where the scary entomologist had got to.

Then I saw them. They were hurrying back along the street that led to their home. Even from my great height I could see how the sunshine on their red hair burnished it. It was a colour that reminded me of something, and with a shock I recalled the lifeless red-golden butterfly in the entomologist's jar. And then, as if on cue, I saw the entomologist himself. He was striding on his long spider legs along a street parallel to the girls. He seemed very purposeful. Had he been on the same street, I might have thought he was chasing them. I flew downward in a spiral, keeping the girls and the strange loping man in view. He was now ahead of the girls despite the lead they'd had. He was after something, I was sure, and it wasn't a butterfly or a beetle, as his telescopic net had been pushed shut and packed away. Then at the next intersection he took a turn that would bring him even closer to the girls. In fact, if he was planning to make another turn at the next intersection, he would meet them head-on.

It suddenly occurred to me that this was his plan. I flew even lower, wondering whether I should warn them. And then I thought of stroppy Suzy. If anything she could handle the entomologist all by herself. The two of them would be more than a match for him.

All the same, I wished I had another bucket of water so

that I could dive-bomb him if necessary. Instead, I hovered, keeping all three under close surveillance.

Sure enough he turned the corner. He was now on the same street, facing the girls, but on the other side of the road. He paused, making sure they were there, and then he started again. It was just as if he were stalking an insect, as though the twins were his prey.

The girls hadn't noticed him. They were still quite a way away and that decided me. The spider man (I was thinking of him like that now) had the advantage of speed, but I was determined that he wouldn't have the advantage of surprise. I gave up hovering at once and swallow-dived down, down towards the girls. By the time I'd landed just in front of them the spider man was still at least fifty metres away and still on the other side of the road.

'Meg!' I called. 'Suzy! Look!'

I pointed across the road, and the girls swung that way.

'It's him again,' cried Meg.

'Oh, for God's sake!' cried Suzy.

Immediately upon seeing that the girls had spotted him, the man stopped. Then he began moving again, but without looking their way. He kept his eyes averted completely. He reminded me of a skinny black cat trying to pretend he wasn't in the least interested in the sparrows on the lawn. He was so obvious, you wanted to laugh. Or at least you would have if he hadn't been so creepy.

The girls had stopped too.

'What'll we do?' asked Meg.

'Nothing,' said Suzy. 'He's probably harmless. Anyway, he can't get both of us. Just keep an eye on him.'

'Tell you what,' I suggested. 'You guys run on home. I'll stay here and watch him. I've been watching him from up high anyway and it really looked like he was trailing you. If he does anything odd I'll shout, okay? He can't see me so I'll be all right.'

'That's a good idea,' said Meg.

She meant it, too. I could tell from her tone that she was anxious.

'I guess you're good for something after all,' said Suzy. But she gave me that little half-grin again, so I guessed she was pleased with the idea too.

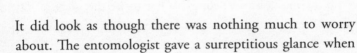

It did look as though there was nothing much to worry about. The entomologist gave a surreptitious glance when the girls headed off once more, but he made no attempt to follow them. I backed into the large green hedge behind me and watched him carefully.

He continued walking, but not at the same frantic pace as before. He had slowed right down to a grotesque tiptoe. When he was almost adjacent to where I was standing, he crossed the road.

He didn't cross diagonally. He walked with unerring accuracy directly towards me. He stood barely a metre in front of me for a moment, gazing towards the twins who were already walking swiftly away. I wondered whether he was about to set off after them with his great loping strides, when he turned again and stared directly at me.

For a foolish moment I thought he could actually see me. Then the moment wasn't foolish.

It wasn't foolish at all.

I realised with a lurch that he could see me, that he'd probably been able to see me all of the time.

His hands reached out and he gripped me by the shoulders.

'I've got you!' he laughed. 'I've really got you! Pinch me! I can hardly believe it!'

'Meg!' I screamed. 'Suzy!'

I turned to look to the girls for help, but already they were far away; almost at the corner and out of earshot.

Then I was lifted into the air and swung under the entomologist's arm.

'Pinch me,' he gasped. 'This has to be the greatest day of my life!'

EIGHT

THE BUTTERFLY COLLECTOR clapped one hand over my mouth and his right arm gripped me tightly against his side as if he were carrying a sack of potatoes.

'Wonderful, wonderful,' he muttered. 'We'll just get you inside and safely out of harm's way . . .'

I tried to shout but his hand completely muffled me. I tried to hit him with my hands and kicked furiously with my feet, but he was holding me in such a way that both arms and legs were only able to flail at the air.

We went only a few metres before he opened a gate and we passed into his front yard. I realised then that the hedge I had been snuggling into was the laurel hedge Meg had spoken of. I had been stationed outside his very house! And the laurel leaves I had been standing against must have been the same crushed leaves he used to kill his butterflies.

He lurched up the path and up the steps to his front door. The house towered above me. It must have been very old, as it had tall windows and turrets and shingled balconies all about it. The door was solid, but it had a leadlight fanlight above it with red stained glass the colour of rump steak.

The entomologist took his hand from my mouth and fished in his pocket for a key. For a brief moment I was able to shout and scream before his hand clamped over my mouth once more. Then the door was unlocked and we were inside. He did not, however, let me go. Instead, he hurried down a dark passage and up a curved flight of stairs with a threadbare red carpet and a dark-stained banister.

There was a landing at the top of the stairs with a number of doors. He struggled with me towards the nearest door on the right and took out his keys again. With great dexterity, for I was wriggling and writhing as much as I was able to, he found the key and pushed it into the keyhole.

The room was large. At first I thought I must have been taken into a museum gallery. Almost every available space on every wall was taken up with a succession of glass-fronted display cases, and each case was filled with row after row of neatly labelled butterflies and moths. All the butterflies, though, looked very dead. Their wings were like dried coloured paper.

One wall of the room was given over to large French doors draped on each side with faded velvet curtains and leading to a decorative balcony that overlooked the side garden. I only briefly took in the window as a means of escape, as my eyes more immediately were drawn to a small free-standing cage in the corner of the room. It would have looked a little like a toddler's playpen were it not for the fact that it was twice as large, it had bars on the top, and instead of wooden dowelling, the bars were made of dark-grey steel.

'This'll keep you safe,' whispered the entomologist as, once again, he drew forth a key and undid the padlock that fastened the door to the cage. He pulled the door open, slung me off his side, then pushed me into the cage, slamming the door immediately behind me. Then, almost in one movement, he slipped the hasp of the lock through the slot and snapped the padlock shut.

'Got you!' he laughed. 'Oh this is my lucky, lucky day!'

I gripped the bars and stared out at his spidery frame. He was shaking with happiness.

'Who are you?' I whispered.

He came close, grinning so broadly that his bad teeth were thrown into sharp relief.

'I'm a Collector,' he said, as if it were obvious. 'Butter-flies . . . moths . . . and now, and now . . . I have that rarest of specimens, a treasure a Collector could only dream about: a loblolly boy!'

I swallowed. He was crowing about me! He had always been after me! And I'd thought he had been pursuing the twins. All the time he had been after me, and I had fallen completely into his trap.

The Collector was obviously beside himself with happy excitement. He could not stand still. He moved about the room, and every so often he gave a little dancing kick in a gleeful jig, and he clapped his hands together from time to time. There was an old roll-top desk at the far end of the room beneath one of the largest display cases. As if suddenly remembering something, he mumbled to himself, and hurried over to it, and pushed up the lid. Then he opened a drawer and began rummaging in it. He evidently found what he was looking for as I next heard a loud grunt of satisfaction and he came loping back towards me.

He reached into the cage once more and I could feel his hands investigating my clothes, feeling my closed wings. It was not nice.

'Don't touch me!' I cried.

'Just making sure of things,' he giggled, but he did withdraw his hands and he clapped them together once more as if applauding himself for his own cleverness.

'How can you see me?' I asked.

'Special glasses!' he cried. He reached up and pulled the funny-looking round pebble glasses off his nose and flourished them about, then flung them back on. 'Now you see him!' he cried with the glasses on. 'Now you don't!' he cried with the glasses off.

I stared at him. 'You could see me all the time?'

He nodded happily. 'Oh, yes. But the skill of the hunter . . . never let the target know you're after it. Pretend you're interested in something else.'

Awkwardly he pulled his glasses back on, fixing them behind his ears.

I stared at him glumly. That was exactly what had happened. Thinking he was really after the twins, I had fallen like a half-blind booby into his trap.

'Where did you get those glasses?'

I'd had no idea such things might have existed. The captain had not told me about them, although he had warned me of Collectors and others who would do me harm.

'Oh,' the Collector said airily, flicking his long fingers

110

into the air. 'I *obtained* them from a fellow Collector some time ago . . .'

Something in the way he said *obtained* suggested his acquiring the glasses had not been entirely honest.

'Why?'

He looked at me in astonishment. 'To catch you of course, silly loblolly boy!'

'But how did you know about me?'

The look of astonishment shifted to one of craftiness. He rubbed his long nose knowingly and chuckled. 'For real Collectors,' he said, 'there is always the beyond, the final all-but-unobtainable. Some call it the sublime, the unsurpassable, the max. It is the *crème de la crème*, the *ne plus ultra*, the nth degree, the holy grail . . .'

I stared at him. He was almost salivating. What he was saying made no sense at all to me, but it seemed to mean everything to him. He gestured around the room at the array of glass cabinets and their frozen contents.

'I have it all,' he said, 'or almost all . . . The most beautiful? I have Blue Morphos, I have Radiant Swallowtails, I have Rajah Brookes . . . The world's rarest? I have Queen Alexander's Birdwing . . . Three of them, actually,' he added with a leer. 'I have everything the world of butterflies can offer – in this world. Naturally, this means I have had to go beyond this world.'

He strode towards me and gripped the bars, staring at me with triumph. 'Look about you,' he hissed. 'I have them all. The trouble is, there is nothing I have that others do not. Until today!' he laughed. 'Until today!'

I shrank from the intensity of his emotion and the gust

of bad breath. I could see now why he was so over the top with delight, but he still hadn't explained how he knew about me.

'But, how . . .' I said.

'How?'

'How did you know about me?'

He remembered the question, this time. 'Oh, among the very top Collectors – among whom I number myself . . .'

He stopped, his eyes glazing.

'I am,' he whispered. 'I am the very top. Nothing can surpass . . .'

I coughed, and he glanced back.

'Among the initiates,' he whispered, 'there has been knowledge of the loblolly boy. Some thought it a legend, some thought it a dream. But in the innermost circle there was no doubt, and special crystal glasses were devised that would separate the light colours that hid you from those that would reveal you. Every now and again you were seen, of course, by a Collector with these glasses, but usually high in the sky and well away from possible capture . . .'

He rubbed his hands together like a villain in a melodrama.

'So long . . . so long . . .'

'What do you mean?'

'I've been waiting years for this opportunity. *Then felt I like some watcher of the skies, when a new planet swims into his ken!*'

'What's that?'

'Keats. *Chapman's Homer*. Way beyond you, you silly little loblolly boy!'

The man was obviously mad. Demented. At the same time, the cage I'd been flung into looked very real and very solid. I began to wonder how long he intended to keep me there. Then I began to wonder why.

'Why have you locked me in here?'

He turned to me in astonishment. Then he began to laugh. The laugh began with a little giggle that sounded like cellophane, then ended with a chuckle that sounded like sandpaper.

'You are such a stupid little loblolly boy. I need to keep you here until I've prepared your display case, of course. It will have to be a big one and it will take some time. Don't you have a brain, little one?'

It was only then that the true ghastliness of my situation began to sink in. I knew I had a brain, but it seemed not to have been working very well lately. I looked around the walls again, at the dead butterflies skewered onto their neatly labelled backing cards. A single pin through the middle of each of the beautiful creatures fixed it to the card. Their wings were spread out so that they looked like tiny technicolour angels. There were large butterflies and small butterflies; drab butterflies and brilliant butterflies. Some had regular triangular wings, while others had looping narrow wings with hanging lobes as if they had been wearing heavy earrings. Each one at some stage had been a small triumph. Found, pursued, netted, poisoned, then carefully mounted. Underneath its outstretched wings, in tiny spidery copperplate handwriting, its name, date and location had been meticulously inscribed.

And this was going to happen to me.

I had been found. I had been pursued. I had been captured.

I knew what the next step in the sequence would be. I remembered how this deranged entomologist had held up the glass bottle containing the golden-red wings and lifeless body of the dead butterfly. The Matheson Gold. And out front he had a tall laurel hedge with enough laurel leaves to poison every moth and butterfly in the country.

What a fool I'd been. I remembered the captain's warning about the dangers of the world and about the people who might harm me. The people who were dangerous. He'd told me about the Collectors. I could hear his deep and serious voice. They might keep me in a cage, he'd said, like some exotic species. Well, I'd met a Collector, and I was in a cage. The trouble was, this Collector wasn't going to keep me there. This Collector was going to put me to death then pin me, wings outstretched, in a glass-fronted display case.

It was utterly hopeless. I rattled desperately at the bars but they were as solid as a prison. As they were only a few centimetres apart, it was all I could do to get my arm through them. To squeeze my entire body through was less than a forlorn hope.

For some time I had been left alone. From far away, deep within the bowels of the house, I could hear footsteps every now and again and muffled bangings. The Collector was busy at something, and I suspected it was building a display case. It was not a very pleasant thought.

I slumped to the floor of the cage. It really was such a hideous quandary. Even if someone came who might have been able to rescue me, they couldn't see me to know I needed rescuing. All they would see would be an empty cage. The people I knew who could see me numbered just four, not counting the seagull: Captain Bass, Meg, Suzy, and Mr Spider Weirdo Butterfly Collector himself, as long as he was wearing his special glasses.

But just then I heard another sound. A scratching at the window. I looked up. It was Suzy. She was standing on the little decorative balcony. Somehow she had scrambled over the wrought-iron railing and she now stood, evidently puffing, peering cautiously in through the glass. Her worried face was red with exertion.

Then she saw me in the cage and her eyes widened. I waved and she waved back. She looked from side to side, clearly inspecting the door from all angles to see whether there was a way in. There didn't seem to be, for the next thing Suzy was shaking at the door, at first gently, then with increasing violence. Luckily, at the same time as she was shaking at the door, the hammering from down below was loud as well, and I hoped the two would cancel each other out. Certainly the door seemed to be giving. Then with a huge yank, Suzy pulled it open by brute force and stepped into the room.

'Hello,' she said, as if finding me in a cage was a perfectly normal event.

'Can you get me out of here? That lunatic locked me in and he's going to do that to me!' I pointed around the room at the dozens of display cases.

Suzy glanced about her, then whistled through her teeth.

'What? Put you in a glass case?'

'That's what he says.'

'That's seriously sick,' said Suzy, looking more intently at the nearest display case. 'How's he going to do that?'

'It's what he's doing now. That's what all that banging is, I think. He's building a case.'

'He's mad,' said Suzy.

'Of course, he's going to kill me first,' I added in a small voice.

'That's even sicker,' said Suzy.

'Well, he's going to . . .'

'Not if I can help it, he won't,' said Suzy determinedly. She strode over to the cage and pulled at the door. The cage, though, wasn't made of dry splintery wood like the French door. The cage was constructed of steel bars and the door was secured by a bolt and a large, solid-looking padlock.

Suzy quickly gave up pulling at the door. She shook the padlock, more in curiosity than hope.

'Where's the key?'

'In his pocket.'

'Just asking . . .'

'What'll we do?'

Suzy looked at me. 'I don't know. I'll think of something.' She said it angrily, but I didn't think she sounded all that confident. There was no way she would be able to get me out of the cage without the key, and the weirdo had the key in his pocket. I could hardly see him giving it to her.

'It's hopeless,' I said. Suddenly I felt even more frightened and very alone.

'I'll get help,' said Suzy with more determination. 'I'll get Mum. I'll get the police.'

'What good will that do?' I asked bitterly. 'Your mum can't see me and neither could the police. It's no crime to have an empty cage in your room. It's wacko, but it's not a crime.'

Suzy slumped again. She wrapped her hands around her cheeks and gave a little sigh. She knew that what I had said was right.

'You'd better lock the door,' I said. 'He could come back at any time and you might end up in the cage with me.'

Suzy glanced towards the door. It had been rather quiet downstairs for some time. 'You're right,' she whispered. 'Just a moment.'

She tiptoed over to it and closed it gently. There was a key in it which she quickly turned. For some silly reason I felt a little safer.

'How did you know to come here, anyway?' I asked.

'Well, when you said that the guy was chasing after us and that we'd better get away, I thought at first that you were right. I kept a good eye on him when he was on the other side of the road. But he sort of ignored us yet still seemed to be prowling, you know? Then I suddenly realised that he probably wasn't after us at all; that he was probably after you.'

I looked at her with new respect. Suzy was one smart girl.

'I mean, it stood to reason. Why would he have been after us? We're just ordinary kids. But that guy was passionate about things that fly, like rare butterflies and moths and stuff. I thought, what if he'd been able to see you?

117

Of course he'd pretend he couldn't, otherwise he'd warn you, wouldn't he?'

I nodded miserably. 'That's exactly what happened,' I said. 'He told me as much. Never let the target know you're after it. That's what he said. The skill of the hunter . . .'

'Yeah,' said Suzy. 'So when we turned the corner, I stopped and looked back. That's when I saw him go over to the hedge and grab you. Meg and I crept back and we saw him bring you inside. We've been looking about the place, keeping out of sight. I climbed up a trellis to the balcony to have a look and there you were. Bingo!'

'I'm glad you did,' I said.

'Yeah,' said Suzy.

Her tone was a little sour, and I knew what she was thinking. She was thinking that whether I was glad she'd climbed up to the balcony or not was completely beside the point. The only thing that mattered was getting me out. Otherwise I was going to be stretched in a display case. Invisible to the world, but dead all the same.

And right at that time, there did not seem to be the remotest possibility of getting me out of that cage.

Unless . . .

'Suzy,' I said. 'If that weirdo were to catch you, he wouldn't put you in the cage with me, would he?'

She looked at me, thinking. Then she shook her head. 'No,' she said, 'he wouldn't . . .'

'Because . . .'

'Because, if he did I could be seen . . . and when Meg told Mum or the police, they would come in and they'd be able to see me.'

'Right.'

'And he could be arrested or something. For kidnapping. Right?'

'Right.'

'Right. So what are you thinking?' asked Suzy.

I was thinking of how I had become a loblolly boy in the first place. I was thinking of the dark garden in the grounds of the Great House and of the barking dogs getting closer and closer and closer. I saw myself there, the boy I had been. I saw the loblolly boy. He had reached for me and told me to jump at the same time. I remembered the powerful energy that seemed to emanate from his dry hand just before I had flown high into the air above the snapping jaws of Mastiff. Then I remembered the blue flash. This was what the captain had called an Exchange.

I had believed I could end my loblolly boy days by Exchanging with Meg or Suzy. They could see me. They could Exchange with me. That was until I'd thought better of it. Now, however, it was a matter of life or death.

'Loblolly boy,' said Suzy. 'What's up?'

I considered the situation quickly. It was a huge ask, but it was my only chance.

'I was thinking that if you were in this cage instead of me, then the weirdo would be forced to let you out. As you said, he could be arrested otherwise. Besides, you'd be useless. I mean, he doesn't collect girls. He collects butterflies and loblolly boys.'

Suzy looked at me. 'You've thought this out very carefully all by yourself, haven't you?' she said sarcastically. 'Loblolly boy, it's absolutely brilliant. Solves the problem perfectly. You come out and I'll go in. Terrific!' She stared at me as if I were completely crazy. 'Hasn't it occurred to you that there's just one small problem?'

I waited.

'The cage! You idiot! How do you get out and I get in without opening the bloody cage?'

'Don't shout!' I whispered. 'It's not stupid. It can be done.'

Suzy looked at me incredulously. 'Yeah? And pigs can fly!'

'No they can't. Not pigs. But *I* can fly. And I am invisible – to most people. This stuff happens.'

All at once the expression on Suzy's face changed. She looked at me with a sudden interest. Her eyes widened. 'I was forgetting,' she whispered. 'Go on.'

'The reason that I am a loblolly boy is that I met a loblolly boy. I was able to see him. When he realised I could see him he tricked me into Exchanging with him. He's now living in my body and I'm living in his. A loblolly boy. I told you, remember?'

Suzy's eyes had never left mine.

'So . . .' she whispered.

'You and Meg . . . you're able to see me. You're Sensitives. That means you'd be able to Exchange with me.'

Suzy's eyes widened even further with wonder.

'How?' she whispered. 'How does it happen?'

'I don't really know. All I remember is his holding my hand and telling me to jump because the dogs were coming. There was a kind of blue flash and the next thing I knew I was flying.'

'That's weird,' said Suzy.

'The whole thing's weird. Everything's weird, but that's how it works. You become a Newborn,' I said. I was thinking quickly. 'Look,' I added. 'That loblolly boy tricked me. This is different. I'd play fair, Suzy. It's horrible being a loblolly boy. It's fun at first with the flying and stuff but, like I said to the captain, in the end it's just like being a ghost. Like being dead. You're on your own all the time . . .'

'What are you saying?'

'I'm saying that if you'll help me get out of here, I'll play fair. As soon as Mr Weirdo Whacky lets me out, as he has to, and I get back to your place, I'll Exchange back again. I promise. I wouldn't do the dirty on you . . .'

Suzy nodded.

'Believe me,' I said desperately.

'I believe you,' she said.

'Well?'

'Okay,' she whispered. 'Let's do it. It sounds completely crazy, but it doesn't look like there's any other way of getting you out of here.'

Just then, as if to underline the urgency of the situation, there was a telltale *thump*, *thump*, *thump* of footsteps on the stairs.

'He's coming!' I whispered in a panic. 'Quick, Suzy! Give me your hand!'

I reached through the bars and seized Suzy's hand. She gripped it and I squeezed my eyes shut, willing the Exchange to take place. Even as I did so there was a jiggling at the door handle. The Collector had discovered that the door was locked. The jiggling became more urgent, then more furious, and then there was a voice.

'What's going on in there? Who locked this door!'

I squeezed my eyes even more tightly, willing the Exchange with my entire being. 'Fly!' I cried. 'Fly, Suzy!'

Then the Collector was banging at the door. It sounded like he was beating at it with his fist. 'Open up!' he shouted. 'Open up or I'll break this door down!'

I felt a welling despair. It wasn't working. At any moment he would burst into the room. I could almost see the door swing open, the flying splinters.

'Fly!' I half screamed, half begged. 'Suzy! Fly!'

And then there was a flash of blue so bright, so incandescent, it penetrated my eyelids.

NINE

I OPENED my eyes. Jumping away from me in a blur of green was a loblolly boy.

'Oh, wow!' said the one who had been Suzy, as she was thrown backwards towards the French door.

Regaining balance, the creature stood before me beaming, looking down and patting at its filmy clothes unbelievingly.

'Suzy?' I asked uncertainly. My voice sounded strange. Different. It was Suzy's voice.

The figure glanced up, and gave a delighted laugh. 'I'm not Suzy! You're Suzy! Look at you! I'm not Suzy, I'm the loblolly boy!'

'But . . .'

I stared at the figure. I might well have been back in the garden of the Great House. Standing before me was the same figure with the same dark-green cape, sage-coloured shirt and leaf-green leggings. The wings, I understood, were concealed in folds behind him. This must have been exactly how I had appeared to Captain Bass, the girls, and to the Collector.

Did I say exactly? There was the same, regular, somewhat anonymous face, but the wide green eyes of the loblolly boy I had met in the Garden had been swimming, it seemed, with all the sadness of the world. This loblolly boy's eyes, while wide and green, were shining with anticipation.

'It worked! We Exchanged!' the Newborn loblolly boy giggled.

'But . . . but I'm not Suzy, really . . . not a girl . . .' I protested.

'You are now! And I'm the loblolly boy!'

So astonishing had been the transformation, we had almost forgotten the situation that had prompted our Exchange. Now I became aware that all the while the banging at the door had been ever more furious, the muffled shouting ever more crazed and threatening.

'Get away! Get away!' I cried. 'The balcony. Fly!'

The loblolly boy gave me an astonished half-wave and jumped through the door. Then I saw him leap gracefully up onto the wrought-iron railing. He balanced there for a moment and then leapt up into the air itself, his wings opening as he did so, and in an instant he was soaring up into the air, higher and higher, as if he had been flying all of his life.

No sooner had he disappeared than there was another series of thuds at the door. This time the thuds came not from a fist but almost certainly from a shoulder.

I was allowed only a moment or two to make some sort of sense of what had happened. The first thing I had to get to grips with was that I was now wearing blue jeans, trainers and a red fleece with a hood. Suzy's clothes. To all intents and purposes I had become Suzy. Or more accurately, I suppose, I had been transported into Suzy's body. She who had been Suzy was now a loblolly boy.

I touched my face. I touched my ears, and my fingers met the little gold earrings Suzy had been wearing. I could feel that my hair was long and gathered in a ponytail.

This was very strange. I was still me. But I was Suzy as well. Except that Suzy would have been feisty, brave, and I was suddenly very, very frightened.

All at once I realised that my brainwave might not have been such a good idea after all. For one thing, I was still locked in the cage. The whacko Collector was battering at the door. It did not sound as if he was likely to be in a calm and reasonable frame of mind when he eventually smashed his way in. As he would. He sounded as though he would be very, very angry. And how much more angry would he be when he discovered that his catch of a lifetime, his ultimate aim in life, a loblolly boy, had been replaced by a very ordinary-looking human schoolgirl? I knew the answer to that, too. He would be much more angry.

I just hoped he wouldn't be crazily, homicidally angry. But I wasn't exactly counting on it.

Finally, just as I had imagined it, the door did burst open in a flurry of splinters. The suddenness of the door giving way propelled the tall figure of the Collector into the room with a lurching violence that sent him sprawling right past the cage, so that at first he was unable even to look my way. His arms were flapping about and his legs flew this way and that in an even more ungainly fashion than usual.

When he did catch his balance and swing around to check his cage, his jaw dropped. He took an angry stride towards me.

'Little loblolly boy! What has happened to you!' he demanded.

'I'm not a loblolly boy,' I said as resolutely as I could, even though my legs were shaking. 'I'm Suzy.'

'Suzy?'

He shook his head wildly from side to side as if there were a stone in it he needed to dislodge, then he swept his strange pebble glasses off and rubbed his eyes. He looked at me once more.

'You're still there!'

'Of course I'm still here. Let me out!'

'But I can see you without the glasses!'

'Let me out!'

'You're the girl I saw in the park with the loblolly boy!'

'Yes, I've told you. Let me out!'

'But where is he? Where's the loblolly boy? How did you get in there?' He was completely bewildered, the anger dying away.

'He's gone to the police,' I said. 'Or rather Meg has. Are you going to let me out or aren't you?'

'Meg?'

'My sister.'

That sounded strange in my mouth. Strange, but not unpleasant. I'd never had a sister, but now, as far as the world was concerned, Meg was my sister. And I was Meg's sister. It was very odd.

'I don't understand this . . .'

'Look, if you don't let me out immediately, I'll scream and scream and scream!' I said, trying to sound forceful and angry.

'I don't understand it at all.'

'Are you listening to me?'

'All my life I've been waiting for this. A loblolly boy would have made my . . .'

'You're not listening to me!'

Suddenly his anger returned. 'What have you done with him?' he demanded. There was a frightening viciousness in his tone. 'What have you done with my loblolly boy?'

For a moment there was a strained silence. All at once my mouth was dry and I couldn't have replied even if I'd been able to find any words to say. Then, just as I thought he might do something really crazy, given the mad glint in his eyes, there was an urgent knocking on the front door.

'Wait here!' he ordered, and then he looked around desperately but, finding no help, left the room and clumped down the stairs.

Wait here! It could almost have been funny. Did he think I was about to leave? I heard the door open and then I heard angry female voices, one deep and one high-pitched. The next thing I heard was the door slamming and then the footsteps hurrying up the stairs once more. The Collector was already fishing in his pocket for the keys as he rushed through the doorway. He quickly unlocked the padlock and opened the door of the cage.

'Get out. Get out,' he said. Then he hissed in my ear, 'You were not in this cage, understand? You only came in here to look at my butterfly collection, didn't you?'

I nodded. To get out of that cage I'd agree to anything. Anyway, what was a little lying compared to acquiring a totally different body? And the body of a girl.

'Right! Right! Now down the stairs with you!'

I ran out of the door and scurried down the stairs as fast as I could. He loped down behind me, breathing harshly. I raced down the hall, but even so he was at my heels the whole way and reaching over my head to open the door.

On the doorstep was Meg (who gave me a relieved grin), and a tall, worried-looking woman whom I recognised as the woman I'd seen through the telescope, hanging out the washing.

'Suzy!' she exclaimed. 'What's this all about, young lady!'

I didn't reply. I bounded from the house and stood behind Meg, trembling.

The woman, Meg's mother, turned her attention to the Collector. 'What have you done to her?' She was very angry.

The Collector shook his head and swallowed. He gave an uncertain smile and said, 'Nothing, madam. Nothing at all. The little girl . . . she was in the park. I collect butterflies, you see. She expressed an interest and . . .'

'Butterflies!' cried Meg's mother. 'I'll butterflies you!'

Then she turned to me and said furiously, 'Suzy, what have I told you about strange men? Just you wait till you get home, young lady!' She turned back to the Collector. 'And as for you, you mongrel, if I hear that you've harmed one single hair on my daughter's head I'll have your guts for garters, you filthy pervert! Butterflies!' she snorted.

Then she grabbed my hand firmly and Meg's hand firmly and marched us down the pathway to the street. Once out on the street, she said to us: 'I'll have to get back to the corner shop now, or Mrs Tombleson'll go spare. You two get home and *stay* home. We'll talk about this later. For a start I want to know why you aren't at school, and second, Suzy, I want to know how and why you happened to end up in that house with that man! You'd better do some pretty hard thinking, my girl!'

'What happened?' asked Meg.

We were in the twins' bedroom. We had walked quickly home, still struck silent by Meg's mother's anger. There had been no sign of the loblolly boy.

'What do you know?' I asked.

'Only that the loblolly boy found us on the street outside that strange guy's house. You'd climbed up to that balcony and disappeared. I got scared when you didn't come back, especially when I heard a lot of banging, so I ran down to the corner shop to tell Mum. We were almost at the gate when the loblolly boy saw us and flew down. He told me you were in a cage!'

'I was,' I whispered.

'Anyway, I didn't tell Mum that or she would have just about killed the guy.'

129

I nodded.

'Anyway, we knocked at the door and Mum told the guy that she had reason to believe you were inside and if he didn't fetch you out immediately she was going to go straight to the police. The guy sort of went white and said there was no problem, that he thought there must have been some sort of a misunderstanding, and that he'd go and get you. Then he shut the door. Mum was just about to bring the roof down when he came back again and you were with him.'

'I *was* in a cage,' I said.

Meg stared at me.

'You were?'

'Where's the loblolly . . . boy?' I said. 'She, I mean he, was supposed to . . .'

Meg continued to stare at me. Suddenly she stepped back, her eyes widening with fear.

'Wait a minute,' she whispered. 'Who are you? You're not Suzy, are you? Where is she? And who are you?'

I guess I should have realised I wouldn't be able to fool Meg, even if I'd wanted to. Twin sisters probably know each other more closely than anybody else. I suppose it was as much as I'd hoped for to get as far as being in the room with her before she twigged. The only reason I hadn't tried to explain the whole situation was that I didn't know whether she'd be able to handle it; it was all so crazy.

I needn't have worried, really.

Slowly, carefully, I explained the whole thing. How, as the loblolly boy, I'd been put in the cage, and how the

Collector was going to kill me then put me on display as the centrepiece in a trophy room full of dead moths and butterflies, and how Suzy had climbed into the room and found me there but try as she might was unable to free me, and how finally we managed to Exchange in order to force the weirdo Collector to open the cage and let me out.

Meg listened to all of this with increasing astonishment.

'So the loblolly boy who told me Suzy was in the cage was really Suzy?' she asked.

I nodded. 'In a way,' I said.

Meg stared at me with wondering eyes.

'She did a terrifically brave thing,' I whispered. 'She saved my life.'

'But if Suzy is now the loblolly boy, how will she get back?' asked Meg.

'No problem,' I said. 'That was part of the deal. We're going to meet here and she and I will Exchange again. I promised her.'

'Can you?' asked Meg nervously.

'Don't see why not,' I said confidently. 'We did it before, didn't we?'

Meg nodded, reassured. Her question had rocked me a little, though. I hoped we would be able to Exchange. But with a sinking feeling I suddenly realised I knew nothing of the process of Exchanging. What if we couldn't Exchange once more? What if Exchanges worked only one way? In that case I could be doomed to spend the rest of my life as Suzy, the rest of my life in somebody else's body, and the rest of my life with that scary, angry woman as my mother.

At the thought of Meg and Suzy's mother I remembered that there were going to be some very hard questions that I'd have to answer if the loblolly boy didn't come back soon.

Where *was* the loblolly boy?

'What's your name?' asked Meg.

I looked at her. Hardly anybody ever used my name, and I never used it myself. In the Great House I'd kept to myself. Most people had called me 'You' or sometimes 'Red', on account of my hair.

'What do you mean?' I asked.

'Your name?' asked Meg. 'You must have a name. I mean, I can't call you "Suzy" because you're not Suzy. And you're not a loblolly boy any more. So I should have something to call you.'

I thought about it. I did have a name. It was on my file, and whenever I'd received a note from the office there was a name on it. 'It's Michael,' I said. 'My name was Michael.'

Meg grinned. 'That's great. I like Michael as a name. Even better, it's the name of my brother. The one who lives with my father.'

'Oh, yeah, I remember,' I said. 'The one Suzy hates.'

'She doesn't hate him really,' said Meg. 'How could she? She can hardly remember him. I can't anyway, so she probably can't. Our father took him off to Australia or somewhere when we were little. We've never seen him since.'

'That's sad.'

'I guess it is. But what you don't know you don't miss. It's probably sadder for him. He's a little older and he's by himself. At least we have each other.'

'He could have stepbrothers or stepsisters.'

'Whatever . . .'

'And you've never seen him since?'

'No. Not once. There's one photograph, though. It was taken at the Sydney zoo. It's a picture of Michael and us standing outside a wombat's cage. There's Michael in the middle, we're on one side, and there's a wombat's bum on the other.'

I laughed.

'Dad must have sent it over when he and Mum were still speaking,' added Meg. 'But they haven't spoken for years now. So we don't know where they are.'

'Where's the photograph?'

'In Mum's room. She keeps it in her top drawer. Do you want to see it?'

I nodded.

Meg gave me a grin and left the room. She was back a little later with a small framed photograph. It was colour, but it had gone sort of orange.

'Here you are. Hurry up, though. I'll need to get it back. We're in enough trouble already and if Mum finds out I've been rummaging about in her drawers as well, she'll go right off the deep end.' She looked at me, grinning, and drew a finger under her chin.

I suppose I knew even before I looked at the photograph what I would see. But the knowledge had been unconscious, way down under the surface. There had to be a reason, a deeper reason, why the telescope had chosen to show me the woman hanging out washing, the red-haired twins, and why of all the people I had seen, only they had been able to see me without special glasses.

The small boy in the photograph was unmistakable. The little face was unsmiling, the eyes were dark and brooding. The twins on his right were barely recognisable. They were very small and were wearing identical red caps with big white pom-poms. Michael seemed oblivious of both the twins and the wombat beside him. The shock of red hair was badly in need of a cut. I guess he was about four years old.

There was no doubt whatever about who the little boy was, though. I'd seen that photograph before.

It was a photograph of me.

Back in the Great House I'd kept one exactly the same in the locker by my bed. The photograph and a grubby white rabbit soft toy were the only things I'd had when I'd arrived at the Great House.

I'd thought at times about the little figures in the red hats. I'd wondered whether they were relations. I'd never known that animal was a wombat, though. I'd always thought it was the back end of a fat dog.

'Something wrong?' Meg asked. My hand had begun to tremble, and I guess I had gone a little pale.

I handed the photo back. I shook my head. My immediate impulse was to tell Meg who I was. That although I looked just like her sister, Suzy, I was in reality her brother, Michael. Her brother, Michael, who had been taken away by her father when he was a little boy. Her brother, Michael, who had somehow escaped from the Great House by becoming a loblolly boy. Second thoughts told me that this

134

wasn't the right time. I took a deep breath to steady myself and was able to give her a little smile.

'You'd better put it back. Don't want your mother to go spare again.'

'God no,' said Meg. 'She'd really lose the plot.'

Perhaps she might, I thought. But Meg herself had no idea how much more complicated the plot had suddenly become.

Meg hurried away to return the photograph. *Your mother*, I'd said. But since I was Meg's brother, I had to face the fact that the woman was my mother as well. It was hard to imagine. I couldn't remember a mother. I had so few memories and none of them were sharp. I must have been in Sydney to have been photographed at the zoo, but I couldn't remember it. I did remember a time before the Great House, a time when there were bright-blue skies, a warm breeze, strange laughing-bird noises, and a white wake of foam spreading out in a growing 'V' behind a large boat. Perhaps that was Sydney?

I couldn't remember a father though.

The thought saddened me. I must have been lodged in the Great House very soon after he'd taken me away. Why?

Meg returned and flounced onto one of the beds. Then she looked at her watch. 'We'd better get the vegetables done,' she said. 'We'd better try and get something right.'

'Okay,' I said. Cutting up vegetables would be a good distraction. My mind was spinning around like a crazy-top.

'I wish that loblolly creature would hurry back though,' said Meg. 'I wonder where she's gone.'

I wished Meg hadn't reminded me of that. My mind began to spin even faster.

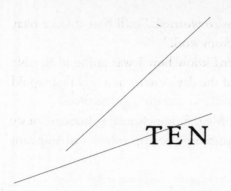

TEN

IT WAS well after four o'clock before the loblolly boy returned. Meg and I had finished the vegetables and had put them into pots, ready to turn on when our mother – I had already begun to think of her that way – returned.

We had gone out into the backyard to scan the sky for any sign of the loblolly boy. There was none, so we sat down on the garden seat and talked.

'Your mother,' I began. 'Is she always such a sourpuss?'

Meg sighed. 'Not always, but mostly, I suppose. Suzy gives her a pretty hard time, and it's been worse lately. They just seem to rub each other the wrong way. I sort of have to be the peacemaker. Aunty Evelyn says she's been that way ever since Dad left and took Michael with him. I'd like her to be happy, I guess, but that just seems to be the way she is.'

I nodded.

'She works very hard and she worries a lot,' said Meg, 'and now and then she flies off the handle. But she calms down again pretty soon. It's the Irish in the family, Aunty Evelyn says. The red hair. Mum's hair was red once, too. I mean she was as mad as hell with us today, but that was really because she was so worried. She'll probably be okay when she gets home from work.'

I hoped so. I didn't know how I was going to be able to explain anything of the day's events in a way that would make any sense.

'That is,' grinned Meg, although just a little anxiously, 'if Old Ma Tasker hasn't rung her up to give us heaps for bunking today . . .'

'There he is!'

While I'd been listening to Meg, I'd half-consciously been looking about the sky. There, far away over the rooftops, I could see a small figure and large, outstretched wings. In the late-afternoon sun the wings shone with an emerald glassiness. Now I pointed in that direction and Meg stood up and shaded her eyes with her right hand.

'It is, too,' she said. 'I wonder where he's been?'

Only seconds later, the loblolly boy was hovering above us and then he descended and landed perfectly just by the clothesline. His wings folded back and he laughed exultantly, then ran over to us and gave first Meg a hug and then me.

'You did get out of that awful cage then?' he asked.

'Oh, yes,' I said a little sourly. I wondered why he-who-had-been-Suzy hadn't bothered to stay about to make sure I had been rescued, and I wondered even more irritably why he had taken so long to get back so that we could attempt the Exchange once more. 'Where have you been?'

'Oh, here and there,' said the loblolly boy airily.

'Suzy!' said Meg.

'Oh, I'm not Suzy,' said the loblolly boy. 'There's Suzy!'

He pointed to me, and then laughed as if he had just made a delicious joke.

'Don't be silly!' said Meg, with a note of real concern in her voice.

'Oh, I'm not being silly,' said the loblolly boy, 'I'm not being silly at all. I've never been more serious in all my life!'

'You've never been serious in your life,' grinned Meg. 'Now stop messing about. Mum'll be home from work soon and you two need to – what is it you need to do – Exchange?'

I nodded. 'Exchange,' I said.

The loblolly boy looked at Meg first, then at me.

'Uh uh. Not me,' he said. 'I'm not going to Exchange. Not ever.'

Then he laughed with delight again and leapt into the air, spreading his wings and soaring high.

Meg and I looked at each other with alarm.

'Suzy!' Meg screamed.

'He can't be serious!' I muttered.

'That's the whole trouble,' said Meg. 'Suzy gets these mad ideas and nothing'll shake her.'

'But . . .' I said.

I saw my life spread out before me. Not as me. Not as Suzy. But as some bizarre mix: me-in-Suzy, Suzy-in-me. It was suddenly very frightening, very confusing.

Just then, the gate clicked open. Our mother had returned.

Meg was right. She had calmed down considerably. Before dinner, I was able to mumble some badly concocted story about feeling sorry for the butterflies the guy was chasing and going in to try to talk him out of going round killing them, but finding him so unreasonable I had to argue and argue, and that I'd forgotten about the time and . . .

'All right. All right,' our mother had said. 'But next time you want to climb onto your white charger just do it in the park, okay? Don't ever go into people's houses again. You don't know what sort of people are out there.'

'I know what sort of people he is,' I said with what I hoped was some of Suzy's spirit. 'He's a complete nutcase.'

'That is my point precisely,' said our mother grimly.

Meg was looking at me with some admiration.

'Don't worry, Mum,' she said. 'Message received.'

I was interested that our mother didn't seem to suspect for a moment that I was anything other than Suzy, whereas Meg had known about it as soon as I'd started talking. I guessed it would make things easier, but at the same time I didn't want to have to keep up the pretence for too long.

'And, anyway,' continued our mother, rounding on us once more. 'What went on at school today? Why were you in the park in the first place?'

Meg and I looked at each other. Meg evidently decided that telling her mother some of the truth was the best policy.

'Bella got out again, and came to school,' she said. 'Suzy and I thought we should take her home or she might be picked up by a ranger or something and taken off to the pound.'

'I see,' said our mother. 'Very commendable. I suppose you asked Mrs Tasker?'

'Sort of,' said Meg. 'She didn't seem to mind . . .'

'I suppose she wouldn't,' said our mother. 'But what happened to her? Mrs Tombleson heard that Mrs Tasker had some sort of a breakdown and was taken away in an ambulance. Do you know anything about that?'

Again Meg and I looked at each other, this time with astonishment.

'I've no idea,' said Meg. 'She might have been a little upset about something this morning. She got all wet at one stage . . .'

'All wet?'

Meg shrugged. 'She could have fallen in something . . .'

'Well, I don't suppose it matters,' said our mother. 'It'll all come out in the wash, I suppose. Now set the table while I grill these chops.'

'An ambulance?'

I was a little worried. Perhaps I shouldn't have up-ended that bucket over her. Perhaps it had caused her to flip completely. I said as much to Meg.

She shook her head. 'Nah, that wouldn't have done it. She was wet all right. But she was just angry. She's a real tough old hen. No, something else must have happened . . .'

We were doing the dishes in the kitchen. Our mother had gone into the living room and was watching a reality show on television, but she had the volume up so loudly we could just about hear the whole thing through the glass doors.

At that moment the outside door opened and the

loblolly boy slipped in. He lifted his arms up into the air like a gold medallist and then flopped them down again.

'Flying is so cool,' he said. 'You can't believe how wonderful it is.'

'I can,' I said bitterly. 'I'm supposed to be you, remember?'

'Jealousy will get you nowhere,' said the loblolly boy cheerfully.

'I'm not talking to you,' said Meg, 'until you agree to Exchange again.'

'That's tough,' said the loblolly boy. 'Looks like we'll never be *exchanging* another word in our whole lives, then.' She laughed at her little joke.

'Where've you been, anyway?' I said. 'You were supposed to meet me here as soon as we got back.'

'Didn't I tell you that?' said the loblolly boy. 'Here and there . . . If you must know,' he added, 'I went to school.'

'School?' Meg asked, suddenly suspicious. 'Why?'

'Weren't we supposed to be at school?' asked the loblolly boy, and then he laughed again. 'It was such fun!'

'What do you mean?' I asked.

'I mean flying is cool, but being invisible is so much cooler!'

'What have you been up to?' asked Meg angrily. 'Is this something to do with Mrs Tasker?'

'How do you know?' asked the loblolly boy.

'What have you done?' I demanded.

'Nothing much,' said the loblolly boy. 'Just got a little of my own back. Payback time, you know.'

'Mrs Tasker?' asked Meg.

'She'll recover,' said the loblolly boy airily. 'She'll probably enjoy a few days' rest in a nursing home or something.'

'What have you done, Suzy?'

'I'm not Suzy,' said the loblolly boy. 'He's Suzy,' he said, pointing to me.

'He's not,' said Meg stubbornly, and with a flash of anger, 'as you well know. He's only stuck in your body until you stop being so bloody silly!'

If that was meant to make the loblolly boy feel bad about what he was doing, it seemed to have absolutely no effect, for he simply laughed again, as if remembering a really good joke. And, in a way, he was.

'You should have been there,' chuckled the loblolly boy. 'You would have laughed.'

'Well?'

'All I did was write on the whiteboard a few times. Of course, as I was invisible it drove Old Tasker spare. When she wasn't looking I rubbed all the work off the whiteboard and wrote up *Tasker is a Basket*. The class was gobsmacked of course, then the kids started to laugh. Of course, Old Tasker didn't have the foggiest idea why they were laughing and demanded to know the reason. Then I added the word *case*: *Tasker is a Basket Case*, and the class broke up completely. Laughing and gasping. God knows what they thought. Magic automatic writing or something. Then somebody pointed to the whiteboard, so Old Tasker spun around and saw what was written there and . . .' here the loblolly boy giggled again at his own cleverness, '. . . and then she went bananas! She demanded that the person who'd written it stand up. Of course, nobody did and then she went even more bananas. She wiped the board clean in a real temper and turned to wag her finger and shout at the class some more. So while her back was turned I wrote *Tasker is a Turkey!* on the whiteboard. The same result. The class laughed even louder and Tasker went spare as she thought they were laughing at her. Eventually somebody pointed again so she whirled around for another look at the board. This time she just about broke the eraser wiping it off. She was sure someone had slipped up and written it there while her back was turned. She turned back to the class and made sure every last person was in their place. Of course that gave me another chance, so I wrote *Tasker is a Tiny-Brained Tuatara with Terrible Breath!!!* This broke the class up completely. When Tasker turned back again she totally lost it. First she sank onto her desk and sobbed for a few minutes and then she got angry again and started screaming and throwing things at the blackboard. Of course she was making such a din that the other teachers and the principal realised that something absolutely crazy was happening and they came and took her away . . .'

Meg and I had listened to all this with growing alarm.

The loblolly boy stopped laughing and looked for our applause. When he saw our horror, he said a little uncertainly: 'You should have been there.'

'I'm glad I wasn't,' said Meg. 'What you did was terrible.'

'It was funny!' said the loblolly boy.

I shook my head. 'It wasn't.'

'It was cruel and nasty,' said Meg. 'What's happened to you?'

'Shut up! Shut up!' cried the loblolly boy. 'I thought you guys would be more fun!'

Then, just as abruptly as he'd come in, he turned and ran out of the door again, slamming it behind him.

'See what I mean?' said Meg. 'Suzy can be great fun but she can be a great pain, too. Sometimes she goes right over the top, and doesn't know when to stop.'

'Or how to stop?'

Meg gave me a worried look. 'Right. Or how to stop.'

We were back in the girls' bedroom. We'd left the curtains open in case the loblolly boy should come back. By now it was dark, although there was a white moon and a sprinkling of stars.

Just then Meg, who'd been standing by the window, said, 'What's that?'

I hurried over to her. 'The loblolly boy?'

'No,' said Meg. 'But something was there. It just hurried away.'

'A cat?'

'No,' said Meg. 'Much bigger. I think it might have been a prowler.'

'A burglar?'

Meg grinned ruefully. 'If it was, he's stiff out of luck here. The only thing worth pinching is our bums!'

I didn't laugh. I hadn't seen anything at all but it did suddenly occur to me that the Collector may not have given up so easily. And if so, that meant he might be out there, and so was he-who-had-been-Suzy.

It was a massive problem.

That night I lay in Suzy's bed, trying to get some sleep, but it was no use. I wasn't Suzy. I didn't want to be Suzy. But unless we could somehow persuade the loblolly boy to stop being so stupid, it looked like I might be doomed to spend the rest of my days wearing her life like an ill-fitting suit.

The trouble was, Suzy seemed to be so much enjoying all the freedoms being a loblolly boy gave her. The wonder of flight. The invisibility. Worse, she had discovered the exhilaration of the power of being a loblolly boy. With a sick heart I remembered the loblolly boy's delight when he'd told us of the awful tricks he'd played on the school teacher and the carefree way he'd been able to dismiss the terrible consequences of those tricks. What if he developed a taste for such mischief?

I knew that sooner or later Suzy would discover that being a loblolly boy wasn't really that great; that a life without human contact isn't much of a life – that really it is a kind of living death. But while she was having such fun and causing such mayhem, this knowledge could take a long while to arrive. And when it did and she felt the need to Exchange again, would she necessarily Exchange with me? Would she want her old life back? I knew she hated it; she'd said so. And if she did Exchange with some other poor person, that would mean I'd be trapped here forever.

The stupidest thing of all, though, was that I'd discovered who I was. I really did belong here. The crabby woman was my mother, Meg and Suzy were my sisters. I just didn't want to spend the rest of my life being my own stupid sister.

As I said, it was a massive problem.

In a way, I did like it here, though. I couldn't remember ever having been in a real home before. As far back as I could remember I'd lived in the Great House. Everything else had been sort of blacked out, or rather greyed out. There must have been a time when Meg's mother had held me in her arms, had made baby noises at me, fed me and changed me. Was it that memory that had made her so sour? Would she want me back? I hoped so. I suspected Meg would. But Suzy was such an unknown quantity.

One thing I did know, however: it was great to taste food in my mouth again. The chops my mother had cooked were wonderful. So were the potatoes. So, to my surprise, was the cabbage.

I wondered whether Suzy realised she would never taste food again if she remained a loblolly boy.

'Meg?' I whispered. 'Are you awake?'

'Yes . . .' came a drowsy whisper.

'What's Suzy's favourite food?'

'Wha . . .?'

'What's Suzy's favourite food?'

'Fish and chips, I suppose,' murmured Meg. 'What a stupid question. Go to sleep . . .'

'Let's buy some fish and chips tomorrow,' I said. 'We could have them in the park.'

There was no sign of the loblolly boy in the morning. When I drew the curtains and looked out at the shabby little backyard I was pleased to see it had rained in the night and that it was still drizzling. I knew the loblolly boy wouldn't

146

have felt the cold, but a drizzling sky dampens the spirits as much as the footpaths. He would have spent the night sitting in a tree or on a rooftop somewhere, with no one to talk to except the occasional damp cat or morepork.

In conditions like these, I hoped, being a loblolly boy might not have seemed so crash-hot.

When I walked into the kitchen to get some breakfast I found my mother already up and dressed in the blue smock she apparently wore at the corner shop where she worked.

'Hi,' I said.

She looked up from her newspaper, a little surprised. 'You're up early,' she remarked.

'Couldn't sleep,' I said. I guessed from my reception that Suzy wasn't exactly an early riser. The wall clock above the fridge said eight o'clock.

'Neither could I,' said my mother. 'It was worry. I do worry about you two, you know.'

I nodded.

'I have to be able to trust you,' she added.

'You can trust me,' I said. I suppose I should have crossed my fingers behind my back. Trust me? I wasn't even the person she thought I was.

'That's just the trouble, I can't,' she said. 'Every time I turn around you're up to some mischief. You should have been at school yesterday. Not gallivanting around in the park with some oddball butterfly collector.'

I didn't know what to say, so I simply nodded again. There was a loaf of bread on the bench so I slipped two slices into the toaster and waited as they began to brown. My mother returned to her paper. While she was absorbed,

I looked at her. I guess I was trying to remember what she would have looked like when I was really little. I was trying to find something to bring back a memory of her. It didn't work. She had a face set in a frown and her hair was greying. Before I could stop myself, some impulse made me ask, 'Where's Michael?'

She looked up, startled. 'What?'

'My brother, you know. Do you know where he is?'

I guess I was trying to find out whether she knew that I'd been kept in the Great House all that time – perhaps she'd put me there in the first place; whether I'd be welcome here if I was ever able to retrieve myself.

'What brought that on?' she asked sharply.

I shrugged. 'I was just thinking about him,' I said.

'Well don't!' she snapped, and then, as if realising she'd been too sharp, she softened a little. 'What's the point?' she asked, more to herself, really, than to me.

'What do you mean?'

'I mean, what's the point. What's done is done. Michael's gone.'

'Would you have him back?'

She looked at me as if I'd asked a particularly stupid question. 'If only,' she murmured.

'If only?'

'If only pigs had wings and little girls could fly!'

'Little girls can fly,' I said. 'Some can, anyway.'

'Yes,' said my mother. 'Once they get a pilot's licence. Anyway, how come you're in such a funny mood today?'

'Don't know,' I mumbled, taking the toast out of the toaster and opening the fridge door.

My mother glanced up at the clock. 'Oh, my goodness. This isn't getting the bread buttered,' she said. 'I'll be late for work if I don't watch it.' She stood up hurriedly. 'Give me a kiss, and don't forget your chores. I'm your mother, remember, not your housemaid.'

And so, before she hurried out of the door, I kissed my mother for the first time in years.

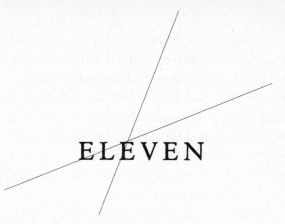

ELEVEN

Two things that I'd established made me feel a little happier: first, it didn't look like my mother had anything to do with my having been in the Great House all those years, and second, I was sure that my mother would have given almost anything to have her son back again.

When Meg got up I was almost cheerful.

'Mum gone to work?' she asked.

I nodded. 'She said I had to do the chores.'

Meg screwed up her nose. 'Usual Saturday. Vacuuming and stuff. That won't take long. No sign of . . .?'

I shook my head. 'No, and it looks like it's been a drizzly sort of a night. It's been raining anyway.'

While Meg set about fixing herself some breakfast, I was thinking. I'd already decided to tell her what I'd discovered after seeing the photograph, even though it didn't really solve any problems. If anything it made them worse. My biggest fear was the one that had occurred to me in bed the previous night: the fear that Suzy might get fed up with being a loblolly boy and run across some other person she could Exchange with. It had occurred to me that Suzy, once she was set on some course of action, wouldn't have the scruples about the problem that I'd had. No, we really had to find a way to make sure she Exchanged with me.

First, though, we had to find the loblolly boy, or he had to find us. From what Meg had said about the dark figure in the backyard last night I was pretty certain that the Collector hadn't given up.

Why would he? Adding a loblolly boy to his disgusting collection was his biggest aim in life. None of our mother's threats would have caused him to deviate from that. They'd have just made him more devious, more cunning, more determined.

Meg was ladling great spoonfuls of cornflakes and canned peaches into her mouth. I sat down at the wobbly table opposite her.

'I wasn't able to tell you this last night,' I began.

She stared at me curiously, her jaw working. 'Mmm . . .?'

'You know when you asked me what my name was before . . .'

She nodded.

'And when I said that it used to be Michael, you went and found that photograph?'

Meg nodded again.

'What I didn't tell you was that I'd seen that photograph before.'

Meg stared at me and quickly swallowed. 'What?'

'Not the same photograph, but another print. I had it back in the Great House. It's probably still in my locker there.'

'I don't understand,' said Meg.

'I think I do. The photograph in my locker is a photograph of me. Or rather, a photograph of the boy I used to be.'

'But,' said Meg. She put her spoon down with a clatter. 'That must mean . . . You must be Michael!'

I nodded. 'I think so. It sort of looks like it, doesn't it? Well, it's too big a coincidence otherwise.'

Meg's eyes were shining. 'But this is wonderful! Michael . . .'

'I'm sure of it,' I said. I told her about the telescope and how it was able to predict the future and that it had immediately focused on this house.

'Why would it do that?' I asked.

Meg was grinning. 'Michael!'

Her joy was infectious. I found myself grinning as well.

'But you never said. Surely you must have known when you saw Mum?'

I shook my head. 'No. I was too small to remember her. I don't even remember our father. I can hardly remember anything before the Great House. All I have is that photograph. And a little stuffed rabbit.'

'Does Suzy know this?'

'How could she? I only worked it out myself after you showed me the photograph.'

'What'll we do?' asked Meg.

'I want to get back,' I said. 'I'm sure our mother would want me back.'

'If you are my brother, I want you back,' said Meg.

'I know. I know that. But the only way I can possibly get back is to somehow Exchange again with the one who was the loblolly boy, the one who Exchanged with me.'

Meg's eyes were shining. 'Of course!' she said.

'I mean, I don't know whether I can. But I have to try. And the only way I can do that is for Suzy to Exchange back with me.'

Meg stared at me. 'Of course. You must.'

'I know, but where is she?'

'Oh, bloody Suzy,' said Meg. 'Why is she such a pain!'

By midmorning there was still no sign of the loblolly boy. I was beginning to worry. We'd finished running the vacuum cleaner over the floor and had made a hurried tidy-up of the bedroom. I soon realised that as far as Meg was concerned, near enough was good enough. We'd thrown the dirty washing into the washing machine and set it going and cleaned up the breakfast dishes.

'Right,' said Meg. 'What next?'

'I'd like to find that loblolly boy,' I said. 'I'd hoped he'd be back by now.'

'I have a plan,' said Meg.

'You do?'

'It might work.'

I looked at her. She seemed a little anxious. 'Well? Tell me . . .'

However, Meg didn't get a chance to tell me as just then there was an urgent banging on the back door.

'Sounds like trouble,' said Meg, hurrying to open it.

It was the loblolly boy. He burst in, shouting, 'Shut the door! Shut the door! Lock it!'

'What's the matter?' asked Meg.

The loblolly boy wasn't nearly as cocky as he'd been the night before. If anything, he seemed very frightened. He'd also forgotten his promise never to talk to Meg again.

'It's him. I can't get away from him . . .'

'Who?' asked Meg.

'That weirdo. The Collector with his stupid net and his bloody jar.'

'So he hasn't given up then. I thought as much,' I said. Then I remembered. 'Meg, remember last night when you said you thought you saw a prowler in the backyard? I thought at the time that it might have been that guy.'

'It probably was,' said the loblolly boy. 'He seems to be able to follow me around. He's out on the street right now, so he knows that we live here.'

'*We* live here,' said Meg, just a little acidly, to remind the loblolly boy of his proper place.

'Whatever,' said the loblolly boy. 'Anyway, he does seem to know where I am. He even turned up at the school yesterday. When I left Old Tasker's room, there he was, over by the elm tree. The creep!'

'That means he must have gone to the school after we left him,' I said to Meg. 'How did he know to do that?'

Meg shrugged. 'Beats me.'

The loblolly boy said, 'Beats me, too, and it scares me as well.'

Meg looked at the loblolly boy seriously. 'Sounds as though it's not all as wonderful as you thought it would be then,' she said. 'And we have to talk. We've got some very important news. I hope it'll give you something to think about.'

The loblolly boy looked up. 'What is it?'

Meg understood the power of mystery. 'I'm not going to tell you right now. Let's meet at the gazebo at half past twelve. If the Collector guy turns up we'll easily spot him and you can fly away somewhere.'

The loblolly boy stared at her. 'What's wrong with telling me now, if it's so important?'

Meg shook her head. 'Uh uh. You fly off and play some invisible games or something. We have things to do, don't we, *Suzy*?' She glanced at me with a tight little grin. I had to admire her. I realised what she was doing. She'd sensed that the loblolly boy was growing disenchanted with being cut off, and increasingly nervous of being pursued by the crazed butterfly collector, and she was determined to make the fear and disenchantment grow and last as long as possible. I supposed it could be called 'softening him up'.

'All right,' said the loblolly boy sulkily. He was very subdued now. 'But I'm not going out the front door. You guys check the windows. I don't want that creep snatching me on my way out.'

'I hope he doesn't have a gun,' I remarked. I couldn't help myself. It certainly had the desired effect. The loblolly boy turned to me with a look of terror.

'Would he?' he asked.

I shrugged. 'I guess he'll get one soon. How else would you bring down a large flying object? It'd be like duck shooting, wouldn't it? I suppose he might have one of those gun things that shoots nets, or the sort that zoo keepers use that shoot anaesthetics or something to put you to sleep.'

The loblolly boy's eyes widened and his wings trembled.

'Anyway,' said Meg firmly. 'Off you go. We have a bedroom to clean up, don't we, *Suzy*?'

'We did all the jobs, Mum,' said Meg.

We were standing by the counter of Tombleson's Corner Shop, where our mother worked. It wasn't long after twelve, and we'd locked up and left the house only a few minutes before. Bella had been on the street again, and had bounded over and followed us, woofing enthusiastically. There was no sign of the loblolly boy and no sign of the Collector. I wasn't sure whether to be pleased or worried about that. It might have meant, of course, that wherever the loblolly boy had disappeared to, the Collector was on his trail. That was the worrisome bit. I'd sort of been joking about net guns and stun guns, but when I thought about it more carefully it seemed to me that the comment hadn't been quite so stupid after all. It probably wouldn't take the guy long to realise that a butterfly net wasn't much of a weapon against a creature the size of a loblolly boy and he'd make other arrangements. He probably wouldn't have too many scruples about damaging the creature, if he was going to mount it in a glass case.

'Do you want an ice-cream, then?' asked our mother.

Meg shook her head. 'Wouldn't mind some money for fish and chips,' she said. 'We thought we'd buy some and have lunch in the park.'

'Oh, I suppose so,' said our mother wearily. 'Goodness knows after the trouble you caused yesterday you don't

156

deserve any treats, though.' She fished in her pocket and pulled out a ten-dollar note. 'Now don't you go buying extra chips just to feed the seagulls and the ducks, mind.'

'Mum,' said Meg with a broad grin. 'Would we do a thing like that?'

'Or that stupid dog.'

'Aww, Mum . . .'

'I know you two like the back of my hand,' said our mother primly, but with a tight little smile. 'No more trouble, now.'

As she handed Meg the note, I gave her a smile. How wrong she was. She didn't know me at all. I was beginning to hope that one day she would, though. Despite her grim face and frowns, I was beginning to like this woman who was my mother.

Despite the early-morning rain, the day had turned out fine. We arrived at the gazebo in the park in good time, and Meg and I sat together on the inner bench and opened the packet of fish and chips. Bella lay at our feet, panting happily. We'd stationed ourselves carefully so that between the two of us we had a 360-degree view of the lawn surrounding the little summerhouse. Were the Collector to burst through the huge spread of the linden tree, we'd have plenty of warning, we hoped. Unless, of course, he'd brought a shotgun with him. I prayed that he wouldn't. There were bound to be laws against firing guns in public parks, even if the targets were invisible.

The smell of the fish and chips wafted deliciously in the

air: a steamy fragrance of fried batter and salt. I hoped it would be enough to entice the loblolly boy to Exchange once more. I had to admit, though, that the smells were so wonderful I wasn't sure whether *I* wanted to Exchange at that point.

'Anyway,' I whispered, taking a crisp golden chip and savouring the aroma of it for a moment before putting it into my mouth, 'what was your plan?'

'It might work,' whispered Meg. 'Especially if Suzy isn't quite so much in love with being a loblolly boy any more.'

I chewed thoughtfully. 'She didn't seem to be,' I said.

'I thought I might be able to persuade her to Exchange with me,' said Meg.

That surprised me. 'Exchange with *you*?' I said. 'Why?'

'Trust me,' said Meg, passing a handful of chips down to the dog. 'You're Michael. I really do want you back. If I can get Suzy to let me be a loblolly boy then I'll Exchange with you again. Promise. Suzy probably wouldn't Exchange with you because that would mean she'd have to admit she'd made a mistake. She hates that.'

'But why would she Exchange with you?'

'Because we're twins. We've always shared things. What's mine has always been hers and what's hers has always been mine. Until this stupid loblolly thing happened, anyway.'

'It might work,' I conceded. I tried to get my head around it. 'It would make things even more complicated though.'

'We have to try,' said Meg. 'We really have to . . . Besides, I'd love to know what it's like to fly . . .'

I looked at her sharply. There was a wistful longing in

her tone I didn't like. Would she, once Exchanged, do a Suzy on me? I didn't know. I did know that I trusted her more than I did her headstrong sister, and I did believe her when she said that she wanted me back as her brother Michael. But at the same time I knew how seductive it was to be able to fly and to be invisible to the world.

At that point there was a sudden fluttering sound and then a slight clatter on the shingled roof of the gazebo. Immediately afterwards the loblolly boy jumped lightly to the ground, folding his wings as soon as he'd landed.

'Fish and chips?' he said. 'I can smell them.'

'They're delicious,' I said, deliberately selecting a large golden chip and feeding it into my mouth.

He stepped into the gazebo, gazing longingly at the open packet.

'You must have realised by now that eating's off the menu when you're a loblolly boy?' I remarked, selecting another chip.

The loblolly boy ignored me then swung his head away and turned to Meg. 'Well,' he demanded. 'What's all this about then? We'll have to hurry, too, because *he'll* be here any minute probably.'

He did not have to explain who he was talking about. Instinctively, both Meg and I checked out the perimeter of the lawn for any movement.

Meg turned to the loblolly boy, and then pointed to me. 'Who do you think this is?' she demanded.

Suzy's old cheekiness returned. The loblolly boy gave a little giggle and said, 'I don't know. Looks pretty much like Suzy to me.'

'Don't be silly,' snapped Meg. 'Be sensible.'

'Just my little joke,' said the loblolly boy. 'Keep your shirt on.'

'I know it looks like Suzy because you two Exchanged,' said Meg. 'But who do you think it was before that happened?'

The loblolly boy shrugged. 'I don't know. The loblolly boy?'

'Yes, but who was he before he Exchanged into the loblolly boy?'

The loblolly boy looked blank. The thought that the loblolly boy may have had a previous existence, as he had, clearly hadn't occurred to him. 'I don't know,' he admitted. 'Does it matter?'

'It does. It really does,' said Meg. 'Did it occur to you there might have been a reason why the loblolly boy sought us out? That there might have been a reason why we could see him and nobody else could?'

The loblolly boy looked confused. He shook his head.

'It's because he was Michael!' said Meg. 'Michael. Our brother Michael. All this time he's been living in this place called the Great House, right in this city, and we didn't know about him and he didn't know about us.'

'So?' The loblolly boy sounded cocky, but I could see he was rattled. I glanced at Meg with admiration; it was amazing how she was handling things.

'So, we could be together again. Suzy, Meg and Michael.'

'But . . .'

'But what?'

'Wouldn't one of us have to be a loblolly boy?'

'Don't be stupid. Of course not. If Michael was Exchanged, all he needs to do is Exchange back.'

'But . . .'

'*But* what now?' Meg sounded exasperated.

'I don't want to Exchange yet. I'm not ready.'

'Not even for fish and chips?'

He shook his head.

'Anyway . . .' The loblolly boy looked at me. 'I don't want to change back into that again. Not right now.'

Meg was looking helpless. At that point she played her last card.

'Well if you don't want to Exchange with Suzy here, what about with *me*?'

The loblolly boy stared at her.

Meg continued. 'It's not fair. Both of you guys have had a go at being a loblolly boy. Why can't I? You told me how great it is. We've always shared . . .'

'You?'

'I just want a quick go. I'd change back?'

'Really?'

I could see how the loblolly boy was torn. They were sisters after all, or had been. I realised that Meg's plan might just work.

Suddenly Bella gave a low growl. I glanced around. Emerging from the cover of the tree was a familiar spidery figure. He was not carrying a shotgun or a crossbow, thank goodness; but he was still carrying a long pole with a big green net wobbling like a battle flag.

'If you guys are going to Exchange,' I whispered urgently, 'you'd better do it quickly. Trouble's just arrived.'

'*Please!*' implored Meg, glancing around and gasping.

'Okay,' muttered the loblolly boy reluctantly. 'We'll change back, mind?'

'Hurry!' cried Meg. 'What do we do?' she asked me desperately.

The tall black figure had seen us and had burst into an ungainly canter. He was approaching quickly.

'Hold hands and sort of will the Exchange. You have to really want it to happen.'

It occurred to me that each time an Exchange had taken place there had been this element of pressure.

Meg seized the loblolly boy's hand and squeezed her eyes shut. I didn't watch them. I was focused on the shambling figure running towards us. He was wearing his peculiar pebble glasses, so he could see the figure of the loblolly boy. There was a sudden blue flash around me and Bella began to bark wildly. The figure stopped in his tracks and shaded his eyes. There was a peripheral movement and I swung around as a figure swept into the air beside me.

Meg was standing there, looking a little stunned.

I felt a welling disappointment.

'Meg . . . it didn't work then?'

The girl stared at me. 'Meg? I'm not Meg. I'm Suzy.'

I stared again. The girl looked like Meg, but so she would. She wouldn't look like Suzy. I was in Suzy's body. I suddenly realised, they *had* Exchanged.

'It worked?'

Suzy who looked like Meg nodded. 'It worked all right. Look at her go!' She stared up at the sky where the figure

162

of the Newborn loblolly boy was rising higher and higher and higher.

Then she looked at me. It must have been like looking in the mirror. I stared back. She looked exactly like Meg.

'This is seriously weird, man,' Suzy whispered.

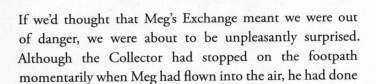

If we'd thought that Meg's Exchange meant we were out of danger, we were about to be unpleasantly surprised. Although the Collector had stopped on the footpath momentarily when Meg had flown into the air, he had done so only to take stock. Then he'd begun to run again. This time straight for the gazebo, and us.

'Oh, my god,' whispered Suzy. 'The man's mad. What's he up to now?'

'Make a break for it, Suzy,' I whispered. 'If you go right now there's still time.'

She flashed me a surprised yet grateful look.

'I don't think so,' she said.

She was right. There was no time to run, really. We could have tried, I suppose, but only one of us might have got away. We both realised instinctively that we were safer sticking together.

Panting with exertion, the Collector quickly reached the door before us. He was very tall and very skinny and his stovepipe black trousers made him look even skinnier, more spidery.

'Go away!' said Suzy, not at all intimidated.

The man said nothing. He looked between us with quick little head movements like a rapid-radar machine. He

163

stretched his arms out and gripped each side of the entrance. It was obvious he had no intention of letting us out of the gazebo. Bella backed towards us, then took a step forward, growling quietly in the back of her throat.

'What do you want?' demanded Suzy.

'You know what I want, you horrible little child,' he whispered, his tongue slithering out between his bad teeth and licking his lips the way a lizard's does.

'Well you're stiff out of luck!' said Suzy angrily. 'Didn't you see him fly away?'

'Oh yes,' whispered the Collector in his sinister way. 'I saw him fly away all right. I couldn't help but notice, could I? When I was so close . . . But I couldn't help but notice, too, that he left some rather precious possessions behind . . .'

'What do you mean?' asked Suzy scornfully. 'You mean these fish and chips?'

'No, I don't mean the fish and chips, you cheeky little swab,' said the Collector grimly. 'I mean *you*.'

TWELVE

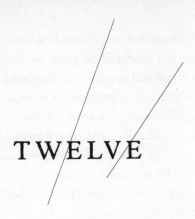

SUZY AND I looked at each other fearfully. The man was completely deranged. I couldn't see through him to the path but I didn't really expect to see anybody nearby. There was unlikely to be anybody even within shouting range. The gazebo was a secret, deserted place.

'I don't really need two of you,' said the Collector. 'One would do.'

I did not like the sound of this at all.

'I think that silly loblolly creature would come back down if he knew that not coming back down would have serious consequences for either one or two of his special little friends,' murmured the Collector, as though thinking aloud. 'You three seem to be as thick as thieves . . .'

The atmosphere had grown heavy and poisonous. Suzy could feel it. Her face had gone white. I could feel it. My mouth had gone dry and my tongue felt thick in my mouth.

'I wonder which special little friend?' whispered the Collector, and his eyes switched between us again with that flickering-radar effect.

I'd forgotten Bella. She, too, was obviously sensing the poisonous atmosphere. The hair on her back was rising. Her low growling grew more pronounced and had turned into a threatening snarl. So intent had he been on selecting one of us as his special victim that the Collector, too, had forgotten about Bella. Suddenly, Bella's threatening snarl turned into a furious barking and she lunged forward, her lips pulled back and her fangs wolfishly exposed.

'No, doggy!' the Collector cried, finally aware of the dog's rage. But his protest was too late and would have cut no ice anyway. He had only time for a panicky step backwards before Bella leapt at his chest. She was probably trying to propel herself at his throat, but the man was too tall. As it was, the full weight of the dog, coupled with the Collector's backward momentum, was enough to push him back and, his hands flailing at the air, he fell in an ungainly heap on the lawn. Bella, letting loose a volley of enraged barks, ran back to stand between us and the Collector, who had ended up on his back like a big black beetle, arms and legs moving like helpless feelers.

'Run!' screamed Suzy.

I didn't need any encouragement. We leapt from the gazebo and raced down the path and under the linden tree. We burst through the branches on the other side and into the wider expanse of the park. To my relief, there were people there: not many, but enough to give us assistance were any to be needed. Bella was at our heels by now, barking cheerfully, enjoying the mad race.

We didn't stop. We kept on until the main gates were in sight. At some stage we must have been aware that the crazy figure of the Collector had scrambled to his feet and was behind us, gaining on us. People stared and stepped out of our way. His long loping footsteps sounded on the asphalt. He was clearly so enraged that not even the presence of the public would have prevented him from doing his worst.

The loblolly boy saved us.

It must have been quite a sight: two girls running in a mad panic with a wildly barking dog at their heels being angrily pursued by a tall figure in black carrying a butterfly net. Suddenly, out of nowhere, a garden gnome appeared in the sky, thirty metres, twenty metres, ten metres, five metres above the tall, gangling figure, a garden gnome which seemed to be pursuing him with unerring accuracy. Almost at the very moment the dark-suited figure was about to seize the slower of the two girls, the brightly coloured gnome plummeted from the sky, felling the figure instantly.

———————

'You know what really annoys me?' asked Suzy.

I shook my head.

'After all that, I didn't get to eat any of those fish and chips.'

'Don't worry about it,' I said. 'You'll get to eat fish and chips again. For a minute there I thought our chips were gone forever.'

Suzy nodded. 'Nice work with the gnome there, Loblolly. So how do you feel about flying?'

The loblolly boy nodded. 'You're right. It's wonderful. Such a sense of power and control . . .'

'Especially when you get to use garden gnomes as ballistic missiles,' grinned Suzy. 'It didn't even break, either.'

We were in the backyard. It was later in the afternoon. Earlier, after the Collector had been laid low by the garden gnome, we'd stopped to wave at the loblolly boy as he'd swooped away and into the air once more. God knows what the small crowd thought we were waving at. Just another craziness in an insane afternoon.

'Let him go,' Suzy had murmured. 'That loblolly boy deserves a proper go.'

We'd turned to look at the very still figure lying spread-eagled on the path, for all the world like a dead stick-insect. I couldn't say I felt much sympathy for him. Whether he was alive or dead, even, didn't really matter to me. I could summon up only a mild curiosity.

Several of the passers-by, seeing the man fall and seeing, too, the bizarre reason for his fall, had stopped to wonder. A couple had fallen to their knees to check his health.

'He's conscious!' one had called. 'Call an ambulance!'

Somebody else had a mobile phone so an ambulance was duly called. Before we'd left the park we'd heard its urgent wailing as it sped towards us.

'What happened?' a woman had asked us. 'Did you see what happened?'

Suzy had shaken her head. 'No.'

'But he was chasing you, wasn't he?' someone else had asked.

'Was he?' I'd asked. 'Why?'

'Where did that gnome come from?' one of the men kneeling by the unconscious Collector had demanded.

'What gnome?' Suzy had asked.

'That gnome,' someone said, pointing. The gnome, too, was lying on its back, in a grotesque plaster parody of the Collector.

'It fell from the sky. I saw it,' a puffing man had cried. 'It was just like it was . . . it was chasing him!'

'It did,' another had said. 'Right out of the sky. Like a giant snowball!'

'Except it was a gnome!'

'Perhaps he had cheesed off the gnome somehow,' Suzy had suggested, and a woman nearby had looked shocked.

But Suzy hadn't noticed. 'Come on, sis,' she'd said to me. 'Let's get home.'

The loblolly boy had been waiting for us when we reached the house.

———×———

Later Suzy asked me, 'Are you really Michael?'

The loblolly boy answered: 'He has the same photograph. You know, the one of Michael with the wombat.'

Suzy nodded. 'So?'

'He's been in this place, what is it?'

'The Great House,' I said. 'It's a place for kids without parents. I've been there as long as I can remember. I only had two things from my previous life: a rabbit and this photograph of me. It's exactly the same as the one your mum has in her top drawer.'

'I showed it to him,' said the loblolly boy.

Suzy, still looking like Meg, looked thoughtful.

The loblolly boy and I waited, exchanging a glance.

Eventually, Suzy said, 'I've been really stupid, haven't I?'

The loblolly boy nodded.

Suzy said slowly, 'You know, it's fun to be a loblolly boy for a while, I guess. But it'd be terrible to be a loblolly girl, boy, whatever, for your entire life. Those fish and chips. I don't just mean them. But no more food at all, ever. And then there's spending every night of the rest of your life perched on a roof or in a tree or hiding somewhere in case that awful bloody Collector or somebody like him has your number.'

I nodded. 'I know,' I said. 'It got to me pretty quickly, too. I guess it's why a loblolly boy spends most of his time trying to find someone to Exchange with.'

Suzy added, 'But it's the invisibility thing that got to me. You know, people need people. People need to be *noticed*.'

The loblolly boy grinned. 'You do, Suzy, anyway,' he said.

'What I did to Old Ma Tasker was mean,' said Suzy. 'I can see that. But I was only able to do it because I was invisible. You know, it's sort of funny. You want people to know that you were the one clever enough to do those sorts of things, but if people *did* know you were the one responsible, you wouldn't do them . . . Deep down, some part of me wanted the class to cheer me on, but the class didn't even know I was there. They will never know I was there.'

'You can't win,' I said.

'What are you trying to say, Suzy?' asked the loblolly boy.

Suzy looked at us. 'I guess I'm trying to say that I think I'd rather be me again. I think being a loblolly boy has its moments, but it's not the way I want to be. Not forever,' she said.

I breathed a sigh of relief.

'Am I glad to hear you say that,' I murmured. I glanced at the loblolly boy. I wondered whether Meg was feeling the same way, or whether she, too, had been caught up in the exhilaration of flight and invisibility.

I needn't have worried.

'It's not the way I want to be, either,' said the loblolly boy.

'Well if that's decided,' I said, 'perhaps we should sort out this mess.'

'Okay,' said the loblolly boy, reaching for my hand. 'Let's Exchange.'

I reached for his hand and closed my eyes. I knew I had to exercise my will as strongly as possible. I pressed my eyes even tighter and began to focus.

But there was something wrong. Some nagging doubt kept wiping away my attempts to focus. The loblolly boy could feel it as well.

'It's not working,' he said.

I stared at Suzy, who was frowning. Suzy who had Meg's face and Meg's body. I glanced down at myself: I was in Suzy's body. I had Suzy's face and Suzy's body. Suddenly I realised what the problem was, and let go of the loblolly's hand.

'Of course!' I cried. 'It's not going to work this way.' The others stared at me. 'Work it out!' I said. 'If the loblolly boy Exchanges with me, I'll become the loblolly boy again and the loblolly boy will have my body. But the loblolly boy is Meg and my body is Suzy's.'

Suzy concentrated. 'Right!' she exclaimed. 'If you two

Exchange, I'll be Suzy in Meg's body and Meg will be Meg in Suzy's body!'

'Crazy,' said the loblolly boy.

'We'll have to work backwards,' I explained. 'Suzy, you'll have to Exchange with the loblolly boy and then Meg will get back into her own body, and then you'll have to Exchange with me so you'll get back into your body . . .'

Suzy nodded, understanding. 'This is seriously weird,' she said. 'It's like some sort of crazy dance.'

It was exactly like some sort of crazy dance, but a few minutes and a couple of blue flashes later everything was resolved. Suzy was Suzy. Meg was Meg. And I was once again the loblolly boy.

It was late afternoon.

'What now?' asked Suzy.

'Between the three of us,' I said, 'we've worked out that Exchanging is not that difficult. Somehow, I guess I need to persuade the loblolly boy who Exchanged with me to Exchange back again.'

'How?' asked Meg.

I shrugged. 'I don't really know. When I was with the captain I learnt that Exchange almost always means a frying pan into the fire situation. I just hope that the guy who's living in my body at the Great House is having such a lousy time he'd be happy to Exchange again.'

'Or?'

'I don't know. It sort of seems unfair that the telescope and the captain should have directed me here without some way of getting me back to being Michael again. I mean, I don't want to be a loblolly boy forever. Besides, there's my mother. I'd never be able to talk to her again.'

Suzy and Meg exchanged glances.

'Yeah,' said Suzy, 'but even if you got to be Michael again, there's still a problem.'

I looked at her.

She continued. 'I mean, from what you've told us, it was only because you came across the loblolly boy that you were able to get out of that place. If you Exchange again, you'll be back in there again. We don't know where it is or what it's called, and you can only get out by flying over the wall. Mum doesn't know you're there. She won't even talk about you, it hurts so much.'

I nodded. She was right. There were two worlds. There was the world of the Great House where I was Michael, and there was the world of my mother and my sisters where I was a loblolly boy. There just didn't seem to be any bridge between them.

'We need to find out just where this Great House is,' said Meg. 'If we knew it existed and where it existed then we might be able to do something. Until we do, we're in the darkness.'

We were in the darkness all right. But what Meg had said did offer a small chink of light. 'I could try to find it, I suppose,' I said. 'It was dark when I flew over the wall and I thought I was flying blind, although I know now that something seemed to be taking me to that little bay where the captain lives. I don't know whether I could find it from here.'

'I reckon you ought to try,' said Suzy. 'There's nothing to lose and everything to gain.'

She grinned at me, and I suddenly realised that I didn't have anything to worry about with Suzy after all.

Shortly afterwards, I opened my wings and lifted myself into the air. There was the promise of a beautiful evening. The late-afternoon sun shone on water, turning pools and lakes into golden mirrors. Houses and buildings basked in the glow and roads gleamed with the quiet traffic that beetled along in a weekend kind of way. I rose higher into the sky to get my bearings. Immediately below me was the house my mother lived in with my twin sisters. Across the road was the gleam of the river wending its way between rounded willows. I could see the school, now deserted, and the large park with the small secret lawn and the gazebo. There on a corner was the red roof and bright signage of Tombleson's Corner Shop, where my mother worked.

I rose even higher. The city seemed to spread in all directions. I only had the vaguest idea of where I might find the Great House. I decided that the best way would be to locate the coast and then try to retrace my flight of the night I escaped. It was easy enough to find the coast. Flying ever higher I soon saw over my right shoulder the great curve of the sea as it licked against the shore. Turning around, I could see the hills indented with bays and harbours, one of which I knew was the bay with the cave houses. I now knew roughly where to head and began to fly in sweeping zigzags on a diagonal from the hills.

It didn't take too long. There, on the edge of the city, I saw the distinctive bluestone towers of a large complex. It was surrounded by a large garden of tall trees, and surrounding the garden was a high stone wall.

It could only be the Great House.

I spread my wings and allowed myself to glide in a falling spiral, down and down. The nearer I got, the more convinced I was. In a matter of minutes I was standing on the wall itself, well out of sight of the house. I knew I was invisible, probably to all but one of the inhabitants, but all the same I felt both excited and cautious. I lowered myself down so that I was sitting and peered into the gloom of the trees. I had spent all I could remember of my life inside those walls and yet I felt nothing. The faces of my fellow inmates were blurred, as were the faces of the Keepers, Nurses, Tutors and all the others who'd pulled the strings I'd been made to dance to. I couldn't imagine how the loblolly boy who'd Exchanged with me would find this life preferable to the one he'd left behind. At the same time, I couldn't imagine how I could possibly go back to it without some very foolproof escape plan in place.

Sighing, I stood up once more and flew up again to circle the building. There were the lawns, the asphalt playing areas with the four square courts chalked at regular intervals. Nobody was out there with a ball or a bat. It was probably dinnertime.

Curiously I looked towards the window of the dorm I had slept in for so many years. The sun reflected off the window, though, and I was not moved to fly down and peer in. I knew that my iron bed would be down there with the green-chequered spread and beside it the little cream-painted locker exactly the same as the eleven other cream-painted lockers beside the eleven other iron beds. I knew that in the locker drawer, along with my spare socks and underpants, was the photo of the sad-faced little boy with red hair and the rear end of a wombat squatting beside him.

I had seen enough. What I really needed to find out was how the girls could locate the building after I'd made the Exchange. Quickly I flew towards the front. I'd rarely seen it: it was out-of-bounds for the children. There was a circular drive in front of the great doors, which led to the lobby and the reception area and the Superintendent's office. The drive left the circle and proceeded down an avenue of cherry trees to a pair of tall iron gates.

I landed on the roadside outside the gates and looked in. There was a sign: *Cherry Gardens*, it read. *Children's Home*.

I'd lived there almost all of my life and I'd never known the name. To me, it had only ever been the Great House.

I looked the other way. I was standing beside a busy road. Further down was an intersection, and I flew down to find the street names. When these were confirmed, I rose again into the air to fly back to my sisters.

THIRTEEN

'IT'S CALLED Cherry Gardens,' I said. 'What a joke!'

'Did you get the address?' asked Suzy.

I nodded. 'Near enough. I got the street name.'

'No problem,' said Meg. 'It'll be in the phone book.'

I wasn't really sure why Meg was so confident. I mean, their knowing the address was useful, but I couldn't see how it would help get me out. I couldn't see the two of them walking all the way across town with a long ladder. Still, it was reassuring that they were on my case. They were my sisters, after all. They'd think of something.

It was almost evening. Already a moon was in the sky and the first stars were beginning to shine. I felt about in the green folds of my loblolly tunic and my fingers found something tucked in there. It was a small piece of paper. I withdrew it and held it up to the little light that was left.

'What's that?' asked Meg.

'Don't know,' I said.

I soon did. It was the scrap of paper that had come with the captain's 'gift'. I unfolded it and read again TO BE RETURNED.

'It's the message that came with the engine,' I said.

'Engine?' asked Suzy.

I remembered that she didn't know anything about it.

'Where did you put it, Meg?' I asked.

'In our bedroom,' said Meg. 'Come on inside. It's getting dark out here, anyway.'

Suzy and I followed her indoors. We went through the kitchen and past the noisy television. Our mother said nothing. I'm not even sure she was aware that the girls had walked through the room. Once we were in the little bedroom, Meg dropped to her knees and pulled out an old cardboard carton filled with soft toys that had been shoved under the bed. She threw out a teddy bear or two and a scrawny giraffe, and there, at the bottom of the box, lay the clumsily wrapped oilskin parcel the captain had put into my hands.

'Here it is.' She handed it to me.

Suzy looked on curiously as I unwrapped the oilskin. I placed the perfect little Hornby train on Meg's bed.

'Hey,' breathed Suzy. 'Who gave you this?'

'The captain,' I said. I explained again all I knew about the captain, leaving out the bit about the two kids and the telescope.

'It's great,' said Suzy. 'But isn't it supposed to have rails and other carriages and stuff?' She picked it up and turned it over. 'And there's a place for a key. Did he give you the key?'

'No. That's all there was. And this note . . .'

I passed her the little piece of paper. TO BE RETURNED.

'Even weirder,' said Suzy. 'It's not even a present, really. Just a loan.'

I nodded. 'That's what Meg said.'

'Wait a minute,' said Meg. 'Remember how you said it was odd that this captain or whatever he is had shown you our place in the telescope and told you to come here and everything but hadn't given you any way of becoming yourself again here? I mean, no clue or anything?'

I nodded. 'Yeah . . .'

'Well, perhaps this engine is the clue?'

'It's possible, I suppose,' I said.

'A key without a key,' said Suzy.

I shrugged. 'If it is, then I haven't the faintest idea how it would work,' I said. I picked up the little engine once more, turning it round and round in my hands. If the answer to my problems was there it was a very murky answer.

'Well, there's one person who can answer the question,' said Meg.

I nodded. She was right.

I would have to go back to the captain. What had he said? *From time to time I'm able to offer solace and comfort to people like you, people who find themselves tricked out of their real existences. Don't look so alarmed, little loblolly boy, I'll do what I can for you. It may not be much. It may be something . . .*

Well, I had been tricked out of my existence, all right. Then in return the captain had shown me the way to a new existence, my real existence. My mother. My sisters. The trouble was, I needed more than the way: I needed to know how to open the door. I was, I knew, not a very intelligent little loblolly boy. Once more I heard the contemptuous grating voice of the Collector: *You are such a stupid little loblolly boy . . . Don't you have a brain, little one?*

179

I had to put my hands in the air, like some outlaw in a cowboy movie. *Don't shoot. I give up.* The problem was too much for me. I would have to look in the back of the book for the answer.

And the back of the book, as Meg was implying, was back in the little bay with the scary Captain Bass.

'Give me the oilskin, Suzy,' I said. She passed me the wrapping and I wound it tightly round and round the engine. Then I tucked the engine into my tunic. 'I guess I'll see you guys later,' I said. 'I'm going to have to go back to the bay.'

I flew through the early evening towards the sea and the hills south of the city. I had no fear that I would not find the place. There seemed to be some sort of homing impulse at work. I was like a pigeon. I was on automatic pilot. I rose above the first hills, covered in houses twinkling with lights and the flicker behind picture windows of television screens. Past the tree-filled gardens and criss-cross of streets to the barer hills beyond, where only the occasional dwelling crouched in the darkness.

And then I was following the coast itself. Steep bluffs, heads and harbours. The surging black sea below me, breaking into white flurries every so often as it crashed over a rock or rose into a breaking wave. There was salt in the air and a low moaning in the wind and my wings lifted and my hair lifted as I rose in the turbulence of the sea breezes.

And then, there below me, was the bay my whole being seemed to have been directed to. I saw the horseshoe shape of it, the girdle of foam as the waves ran up the black sand, and the dark shapes of the cottages built into the caves. There was a faint yellow light emanating from the shack nearest the sea. The captain was clearly still awake, drowsing, perhaps, in his large rocking chair with a pipe at one side and a tumbler of dark rum and green-ginger wine by the other.

I did not want to knock on his door this late at night. Instead I found a ledge high on the cliffs surrounding the bay. It seemed safer somehow. I leaned my back against the rock wall and closed my eyes. The distant sound of the waves lulled me into a dreamless sleep.

I opened my eyes the next morning to warm sunlight and the soft tickle of an early-morning wind. I stretched and sat up. The sea was a hoarse whispering in the distance and every now and then a gull would cry. Standing up on the ledge, I gazed at the little bay below. There was a curl of smoke spiralling from the chimney of the captain's shack, so I guessed that he was up and probably already frying his egg and bacon or a fillet of butterfish.

At first I thought the bay was as deserted as usual. But then I noticed an oddity. There was a small yellow tent with a green fly pitched in a small paddock at the end of the narrow shingle road, with a beaten-up little black Volkswagen parked beside it. Apart from that, though, nobody.

After checking to make sure the engine was still wrapped against my side, I leapt into the air and then glided in a single swoop over to the rocks surrounding the captain's little house.

I landed by the shell-strewn path that wound between the black rocks leading to the captain's door and ran lightly up the path. His door was open, and the wafting fumes of bacon told me that my first guess had been correct.

'Captain Bass?'

I stood at the open door. The captain was sitting at his oak table, a large knife in one hand and a small fork in the other.

'Little loblolly boy! This is an unexpected pleasure!'

It was somehow good to hear his booming voice again. It was powerful and I immediately felt that sense of protection once more after the anxieties of the last couple of days. I looked inside the room and it was just as it had been last time: there was the rocking chair with the captain's knitting left in an untidy heap on the seat, the bed, the table, and on the mantelpiece the glint of the brass telescope.

'Come in! Come in!'

I stepped inside. The captain stood up and came over to me. He reached down and, with one huge hand, lifted my chin up to study my face. 'Ah,' he said. 'Still the same little loblolly boy. You haven't Exchanged, then?'

I gave him a weak little grin, and shook my head. 'Sort of,' I mumbled. 'I have and I haven't . . .'

The captain laughed. 'There sounds a story there,' he said. 'I must hear all about it.'

I swallowed. I wasn't sure that I wanted to tell the captain all about it. Part of me felt he knew all about it anyway, and another part said that with only my version of the story it somehow wouldn't be the real story.

'I met my sisters,' I said.

'Sisters, eh?' the captain said. 'Nasty little things, sisters. I got rid of mine as soon as I could.'

'I don't want to get rid of these ones,' I said. 'I like them . . .'

'Do you, little loblolly boy, do you?'

I nodded.

'Well, I suppose there's no help for you, then,' he said.

I didn't reply. I suspected he was teasing me, but I wasn't sure.

'Did you really have sisters?' I asked.

I wondered at first whether I'd been too cheeky, whether I'd crossed the line. The trouble was, with the captain you never quite knew where the line was. I knew so little about him, but I did know enough to know he was unpredictable and powerful; unpredictably powerful and powerfully unpredictable. I knew too that he was strangely a creature both of the real world and of my loblolly world. He could see me and talk with me and seemed to know all about me. He was able to tell the difference between the loblolly boy I was and the loblolly boy who had Exchanged with me. At the same time, unlike me, he had a fierce appetite and loved nothing better than a greasy fry-up of bacon and eggs and fried bread.

He considered my question. 'Sisters? I suppose I must have. When you've lived as long as I have you've sort of had everything.'

I pushed my luck. 'How long *have* you lived, Captain Bass?'

He looked at me shrewdly. 'Do you mean in years?' he asked.

It was a silly response, I thought. How else could you measure a lifetime except in years?

'I don't understand what you mean,' I said.

'Well, for one like me,' he said slowly, 'and indeed, for one like you, little loblolly boy, years are quite immaterial. We do not age, we just *are* . . .'

Again, I didn't really understand.

'Just are?' I asked.

He nodded.

It was then I decided to risk it all. I asked the big one. 'Well,' I whispered, 'in that case, what *are* you?'

Captain Bass looked at me gravely. He pushed his peaked cap back on his shock of white hair and sighed. 'It's not a question of what I *am*,' he said. 'It's a question of what I've *done* and what I *do*. I've been, of course, many things: a seafaring man on a dozen seas on myriad ships of all shapes and sizes and in all weathers; a smuggler, a fisherman, a lighterman, a wherryman and, I'm bound to say, at times a piratical buccaneer. I've sailed with all manner of crews and complements: lascars and rascals; flesh-filled and skeleton . . .'

'Skeleton?'

'You must have heard of skeleton crews?'

I had, but not in the sense I feared the captain meant.

'Coast ships and ghost ships and bottommost ships . . .'

I shivered.

184

'But since I've been a lubber on land I've had the task of looking out for the loblolly boys.'

I stared at him.

'So since then I've measured my life in loblolly boys.'

'Loblolly boys?'

'I imagine I've known hundreds . . .'

'Hundreds? There are hundreds of us?'

'Yes, hundreds . . . but your tense is wrong. There have been hundreds of loblolly boys, but always the same loblolly boy and always different. It's been my part, when they make their way here, and they always make their way here as Newborns, to offer what I can and say what I must. It is,' he added dryly, 'interesting work.'

'I see,' I whispered.

'I'm sure you don't,' he said matter-of-factly. 'However, I will say this for you, little loblolly boy: you are a little different. I have hopes for you.'

'Hopes?'

'I hope you may be the one who finally reverses the nonsense,' he said.

As if suddenly aware he may have said too much, he glanced over his shoulder to the remains of his breakfast. 'Well,' he said. 'As wonderful as it is to see you so unexpectedly, you'll notice that you've interrupted my small repast. If you don't mind, I'll return to it before it gets all cold and congealed. I do like a rasher of bacon, but not cold and congealed . . .' He turned abruptly and sat back down at his table and began to eat again. His table manners hadn't improved. Before he had finished, his whiskers were shiny with bacon fat and there were droplets of drying egg yolk sprinkled over his seaman's jersey. Finally, he finished what remained of his meal by swabbing around the plate with a crust of brown bread. He shoved this into his mouth and then looked up at me once more.

'There's a reason I'm pleased you've come,' he said. I waited. He seemed to be on the verge of telling me something important. The captain glanced down at his dirty plate and the crumb-splattered table. 'Because you'll be able to clean up these dishes for me while I go and check my pots,' he said. 'There's a cloth in the sink and a piece of yellow soap in the drawer. You'll have to shave it.'

Then he gave me a wolfish grin, stood up, and strode out of the room.

I found an old carrot peeler and scraped shavings from the yellow soap. I put some water in the old black kettle and put it on the hob. While I was waiting for it to heat up I glanced around the room once more. Of course, my eyes were drawn to the telescope. It was very seductive, but I firmly resisted the temptation even to reach over and touch it. I knew how it could bite. I left it there to glint in the early-morning sun.

Eventually, the water boiled and I poured it over the soap shavings to build up a cleansing foam in the sink. I fetched the captain's greasy plate, knife and fork and dropped them into the water.

I was just wiping the plate with the captain's grey and evil-smelling dishcloth when I heard footsteps approaching the door. It had hardly occurred to me that Captain Bass hadn't taken long to check his crab pots when I heard a familiar voice – a voice that sent a flush of terror through me.

'Fancy meeting you here, little loblolly boy. I can't begin to describe how wonderful it is to find you once again!'

I whirled around and there, gangling in the doorway with an evil grin, his ridiculous pebble glasses, and a large bandage wrapped around his head, stood the Collector. He was carrying a coiled rope and an ancient but heavy cricket bat.

I stepped back in fright.

'No!' I cried.

'The word, unfortunately, is not *No* but *Yes! Yes! Yes!*' he laughed, his blackened teeth bared like fangs. He swung a coil of the rope towards me, raising the cricket bat as he did so. I froze. I sensed that if I moved he would have swung the bat and clocked me one, but that if I didn't move I'd only be lassoed. All in all, I felt I'd rather be roped than smashed with a bat.

So, I was roped.

The Collector pulled at the rope and I felt it tighten about my chest. He strode towards me and swung the rope round and round so that I was trussed solidly.

Suddenly he kicked out at me and, foot-tripped, I fell down, as rigid as a skittle.

'So!' he grunted, breathing heavily with the effort. 'You thought you'd get away, did you? You didn't really think a plaster gnome would stop me, did you, you silly little loblolly boy?'

'How did you find me?' I gasped.

It was crazy. I'd flown here in the darkness. I'd slept the night on a ledge high on the cliffs. How could this maniac have possibly known where I'd gone? At the same time I remembered Suzy's fright in the morning. When she'd been a loblolly boy she'd been amazed and scared by how the Collector seemed to always know where she was. He'd been at the school. He'd found our house. He'd been waiting about the street. Finally, he seemed to know that we were in the gazebo in the park. These couldn't have been just lucky guesses.

'Oh, little loblolly boy,' he sighed. 'Silly little loblolly boy. You were far too precious a possibility for me to take for granted. I made jolly sure once I had you in the cage that I had a homing device implanted. Listen!'

Out of his back pocket he took a small silvery metal machine that looked a little like a cell phone. He held it up and I could see it blinking with a strong red light and hear it beep-beep-beeping excitedly. It was then that I remembered his reaching into the cage and feeling about my clothes. He must have clipped something to me then.

At that point I began to scream.

I screamed as loudly as I knew how. The scream must have come out as a terrifying, terrified howl.

'Captain! Captain Bass!'

'Shut up!' the Collector hissed, looking about him in alarm.

'Captain Bass! Captain Bass!'

I knew that the captain probably wouldn't be able to hear me. I didn't care. All I wanted to do was to make as much noise as possible, noise and more noise, a screaming wind of noise, as if all that noise might drive the Collector from the little house in a gale of decibels.

The noise certainly unnerved the Collector. He looked around wildly, then with a satisfied grunt snatched up one of the captain's ugly-looking fish-gutting knives. The knife and two others had been lying by the fireplace waiting to be sharpened on the large whetstone the captain kept beside his rocking chair.

The Collector lurched over and brandished the evil curved blade before my eyes.

'If you don't shut your mouth this instant, I will take great delight in shutting it for you,' he whispered evenly.

I sucked in my breath, ready to scream again, and then I saw the Collector's eyes magnified behind his pebble glasses. They were crazed and angry. And utterly convincing. I realised, with a sickening lurch, that he was serious.

I forced myself to be quiet. I let the air slip silently from my lips and stared up at the man.

'What are you going to do?' I whispered.

'What a silly question,' he replied.

Gradually things grew calmer.

I lay there, frightened out of my wits and at the same time furious with myself. How could I have imagined that we had checkmated the Collector? I knew his passion. Why did I think it could be thwarted by a brightly painted plaster gnome? I had been so stupid.

Even when Suzy had given me everything I needed to know, somehow I hadn't twigged that there had to be some sort of homing device.

I had no idea what to do. At any moment the Collector would probably sling me up over his shoulders and take me away. I now realised that the little tent I'd seen that morning and the old black Volkswagen were already waiting for me.

The captain was probably still out of earshot. I was certain the Collector would have made sure of that. And if I did shout, the Collector would bundle me away all the faster. The best thing, I decided, was to try to delay him as long as possible.

'Was that your tent?' I asked.

He nodded, looking around the captain's room. He was probably looking for a large sack.

'Do you know the old man?' he asked. I shouldn't have been surprised that he'd been able to see Captain Bass. His glasses probably worked for the captain as well.

'It's Captain Bass,' I said.

'Captain Bass, eh?'

'He's an old sailor.'

'I suppose he would be with a name like Captain Bass . . .'

I didn't reply.

'And can he see you?'

'Oh yes,' I said, thinking swiftly. Suddenly I had an interesting idea. 'He can see all of us loblolly boys,' I said carelessly.

The Collector stiffened. He stared at me. 'What did you say?' he asked quietly.

I pretended to be flustered. 'I meant . . .'

'I distinctly heard you say *all of us loblolly boys*,' the Collector said. 'You did, didn't you?'

'I didn't mean . . .'

'Yes you did!' snapped the Collector. 'I heard you. What loblolly boys?'

I didn't answer for some time. *Let him stew*, I thought. Then slowly, as if reluctant to admit it, I said, 'The other loblolly boys in the bay. Why did you think I came back here, anyway?'

The Collector looked away quickly as if gauging how much time he had. Then his whole being seemed to plump a little, as if he had discovered a wallet stuffed with fifty-dollar notes. He turned back to me. 'How does the captain see you boys? Does he have glasses like mine?'

I shook my head, then I glanced meaningfully at the telescope, and quickly looked away as if I had made a blunder. The Collector had followed my gaze and instantly noted the guilty way I'd averted my eyes from the telescope. He stared at it greedily, his eyes narrowing with triumph. 'So . . .' he breathed. 'The telescope . . . I suppose I should have guessed.'

'No!' I blurted. 'You mustn't look through it. The captain gets very angry if people look through his telescope!'

That completely convinced the Collector. He gave me a look of scorn and hissed, 'Oh, be quiet!'

I held my breath, and rolled over. He'd looked as though he was about to kick me anyway. All the same, I did look over my shoulder to see what he would do next. I wasn't disappointed. He marched to the door and looked quickly right and left. Satisfied there was no sign of the captain, he came back into the room and strode back to the telescope. Before he reached for it, he took the knife with his left hand. He wasn't taking any chances.

He reached for the telescope.

'Don't!' I cried.

My cry had the desired effect of encouraging him. He seized the telescope and strode back to the doorway again. Then, after pulling the telescope to its full extent, he lifted it to his eye and swung it left and right.

Curiosity overcame me.

'What can you see?' I asked. 'Any loblolly boys?'

'Not one,' he cried. 'But I can see the most wonderful white butterfly. It's . . .'

There was a clatter as the telescope dropped to the ground. There was a second clatter almost immediately. The gutting knife, too, had fallen. The Collector had disappeared.

I rolled over again so that I could see better.

The telescope lay on the ground, still rolling slightly to the left and then to the right.

In the shaft of morning sunlight that shone through the doorway, a large white butterfly was fluttering in an agitated and confused kind of way.

It seemed a long, long time before the captain returned, but finally I heard his solid, clomping footsteps outside the shack. Then there he was, standing in the doorway with a wet sugar bag in one hand. There were things moving in the sugar bag.

'Well, well, well,' he said, looking at me. I hadn't been able to wriggle free of the ropes; I still lay there, trussed like a turkey and immobile as a clothes peg. 'What have we here?'

'We've had a visitor,' I said.

'I can see that,' he said. 'I'd be very surprised if you'd managed to tie yourself in knots like that all by yourself!'

'Could you untie me, please?'

The captain dropped his sack and stepped inside.

'A cricket player, I see,' he remarked cheerfully, noticing the cricket bat lying on the floor. He knelt awkwardly by my side and untied the knot, then unrolled me like a floor mat. 'Everything all right?'

'I'm okay,' I said, standing up and dusting myself down.

'And what happened to our opening batsman?' asked the captain, looking about curiously. 'Leg before wicket or clean bowled?'

I was able to give him a little grin. 'He was caught out,' I said.

'Caught out?'

'By the telescope,' I said.

The captain nodded. 'Succumbed to temptation, did he? And what did he see, any idea?'

I pointed to the doorway. Just outside, the butterfly was still fluttering about in its somewhat dazed way. 'He saw a butterfly,' I said. 'That one, I guess . . .'

'Mmm,' said the captain. 'A white butterfly. Nasty little things.'

He took a step towards it, then stepped right outside, waving his hands.

'Shoo! Shoo! Stay away from my cabbages!'

Then he came back inside. I couldn't get over how the Collector, who had loomed so large and frighteningly in my life these last few days, had been reduced to something so harmless you could drive it away with a flick of your fingers.

The captain glanced at me, pulling thoughtfully at his bushy white beard. 'You knew him, I take it?'

I told the captain all about the Collector. From the first. I reminded him how I had seen the Collector through the telescope and then I told him how I'd seen him in the park. I told him how he'd put me in a cage and wanted to mount me in a glass case. In telling him all of this, of course, I had to tell him about Suzy and Meg and how both the girls had briefly been loblolly boys and how the Collector had pursued us all.

'Well, little man, I can see you've had quite a few adventures. But I'm still a little unsure why you've come back to the bay, especially when you do seem to have found your family.'

'I've found them all right. But I'm still a loblolly boy,' I said.

'I can see that,' said the captain.

'I want to be me again!'

'That's a laudable ambition. But how can I possibly help?'

'When I left you gave me a gift.'

I pulled out the little engine and unrolled the oilskin. 'This. I thought you may have given it to me as some sort of a key. Something to help me. But I'm stumped.'

The captain picked up the engine. It looked tiny cradled in his large hands.

'There was a message with it, remember?' I pulled out the little scrap of paper and held it out to him. There was the message: TO BE RETURNED.

The captain looked at me, but not unkindly. 'I can read it,' he said.

'Well, here it is. I've returned it. Now what?'

Gently, the captain handed the engine back to me. 'Silly little loblolly boy,' he said. 'Whatever made you think you had to return this to me? It's not my engine!'

I stared at him. 'Not yours . . . but . . .'

'It was never my engine,' the captain said. 'I wanted you to return it though. I thought he'd want it back one day.'

'Who?'

'When, like you, he learnt that the fire was worse than the frying pan.'

'*Who?*'

'Can't you guess, little man?' the captain said. 'The loblolly boy. Your loblolly boy. The one who Exchanged with you.'

FOURTEEN

So, in order to return the engine and meet again the boy who had stolen my life, a few days later I flew back to the Great House. Or Cherry Gardens, as I now knew it liked to call itself.

I had been keen to leave earlier but, 'Stay with me for a time,' the captain had said. 'It's too soon right now . . .'

I'd had no idea what he meant, or how he knew this, but, although reluctant, I agreed. The captain was right. The task I had to do was too important for me to stuff up by being hasty.

Those days were pleasant enough, although I was in considerable turmoil. The day-to-day life of the bay was just a prelude, I knew, to the huge Unknown that lay before me, and that Unknown occupied most of my thoughts. All the same, I accompanied the captain as he stomped along the beach or clambered along the rocky shore to the headland to check his pots. Sometimes I would fly above him, sometimes I clambered along with him. Sometimes, too, we passed by a basking seal or perhaps a group of seals and they would look at us with eyes both sad and a little wary. They did not bark or slip away into the water though. I guess they were used to the captain's regular coming and going. Try as I might, I could not tell which of the seals, if any, were the two kids, Veronica and Jason. I hoped they were happy enough.

On the outside, the captain seemed the same: bluff, gruff and slightly scary. His routine was the same. Huge fry-ups in the morning, and grilled fish at night. After his dinner he would settle into his huge chair with a tumbler or two of dark rum and green-ginger wine and click away at his knitting.

'What are you knitting?' I asked at one stage.

'Fisherman's rib,' he grunted.

That didn't make much sense. 'Why are you knitting a rib?' I asked.

He glanced over to me, cocking a bushy eyebrow in exasperation. 'I'm not knitting a rib, silly loblolly boy,' he said. 'You grill a rib.'

'But you said . . .'

'Fisherman's rib is a style.'

I saw. 'But what is it you're making?' I persisted.

'Why, a seaman's jersey,' he muttered. 'What else?'

'It seems to be taking a long time,' I observed, realising too late that I was being a little cheeky.

This time he cocked both eyebrows at me and then stood up abruptly. He strode to a cabinet on the far wall and flung open the door. There were probably twenty navy-blue seaman's jerseys there, all neatly folded.

'Long time, indeed!' he humphed, returning to his chair. 'You don't know the meaning of the word time!'

That was unfair. It seemed to me I was too aware of time.

I said the captain was the same gruff captain on the outside. But I did sense a growing softness underneath. I guessed this was because we both knew that when I left, although the loblolly boy would continue, this *particular* loblolly boy would be no more.

That is, if things went according to plan. A rather big 'if'.

Eventually, though, the time did come.

One morning, the captain put out his large hand and shook mine. 'My job this morning is to check my pots, but you, little loblolly boy, have a different task.'

'Is it time?'

He nodded. 'It is time to say goodbye.'

He didn't say it though. He simply gave a half-wave, then abruptly turned and began to make his way towards the rocks.

So it was that I left the coast and the hills behind me and once more found myself traversing the edge of the city. I had a much better idea of where I was heading now and it was not too long before I was able to make out once more the bluestone towers and mullioned windows of the Great House.

I hoped I was doing the right thing. In theory, it was easy. Find the boy who'd taken my life, Exchange, and then find my way out of the Great House and back to my mother, Suzy and Meg.

I'd been focusing so much on how wonderfully surprised they'd be, I'd been envisaging with such anticipation how terrific it would be knocking on the door, and having it open on their astonished and delighted faces, that I'd kind of glossed over the other bits, the hard bits, the impossibly hard bits.

Now, hovering above the dark walls and slate roof of the Great House, the awful reality came back.

I remembered how terribly fearful a place it was.

Cherry Gardens?

What a sick joke that name was. The place was a prison, really. A prison for discarded kids. I knew that now. *Lodge your unwanted kid with us and we'll make sure it'll never trouble you again . . .*

Why had my father done it? To please himself? To please his new girlfriend? To punish my mother? All of these?

It didn't matter in the end. What would matter was getting out.

Kids had tried before, but the Keepers had always fetched them back.

The one thing I would have in my favour this time was that I had somewhere to go.

I swallowed, and swooped in descent. Even the air seemed grimmer in this awful place.

Almost the largest tree to the side of the house proper was a pin oak. Usefully, too, it was not that far from the window where my dormitory was housed. I landed in the upper branches of it, in order to plan my strategy. There were, of course, several difficulties. Not the least was finding the boy who was living in my body so that I could speak to him, probably in some private place, just as he had sought me out to speak in the safety and darkness of the garden.

Then there was the problem of how to convince him that Exchanging with me was a good idea. God knew what terrible situation had driven him to Exchange. Why would he want to be a loblolly boy again? But perhaps he might. Like me, he might want to find himself again. Suddenly I could see a whole lot of dominoes falling backwards. Domino loblolly boys. Why would any of these dominoes want to cooperate just so that I could become myself again?

It was mind-bogglingly confusing.

The only hope I had was the one the captain had offered. That everybody had learned the lesson that the frying pan was better than the fire. That the grass is usually browner on the other side of the fence.

That wasn't much of a hope.

For all I knew, the boy who now had my face, my red hair, my body and my name might be just loving it here, might be having the time of his life. He could have made the friends I never made, be enjoying the ghastly food, having a ball in the classroom with the sarcastic Masters and Mistresses, loving the Keepers and taking Mastiff for long, fun-filled walks around the boundary wall.

But then again, pigs might fly, as my mother had said.

Of course, there had been an answer to that.

Loblolly boys could fly.

I scratched the back of my head.

How had my loblolly boy made contact?

He had found me in the garden.

Of course, at the time I'd thought that I had found him, but I realised now he had almost certainly set the meeting up. He had been in a lonely dell, apparently sleeping. I remembered, though, that his green eyes had been open. Expecting me, obviously. He must have known I was a Sensitive. And he had arranged other meetings – but never when others were around, he had made sure of that.

Clearly I must do the same. That meant I was likely to have a long wait until dusk and then until lights out. Somehow at that point, as he had, I might be able to draw him to the window, persuade him somehow to come out.

I settled back into the arms of a large branch as the speckled light from the leaves gently dappled over me. From far below I could hear voices from time to time. Shouts of children, the curt voice of a Keeper every so often, or a fusillade of barking from a dog. These noises were muffled by leaves and distance, however, and strangely hypnotic; sleep-inducing.

The problems continued to nag me though and kept me from succumbing completely to drowsiness. I ticked through the solutions I'd planned to the problems I'd so far considered. All in all, I thought I'd located answers to most of them. Find the boy (easy), talk to the boy (easy), persuade the boy to Exchange (very difficult), persuade the boy to Exchange with the help, somehow, of the engine (promising).

But then I crashed right into that large boulder of the problem I'd only just begun to consider.

It was this: what would happen once I'd Exchanged with the red-haired boy? Answer: I'd be Michael once more, an inmate of the Great House. How would I get out and back to my mother, Suzy and Meg?

Answer: I couldn't. I'd be back in the dorm and the exercise room and the classroom and the compound and the *yes sir no sir three bags full, sir.*

I'd be trapped, just as I had been all my life.

I'd only half-joked that Suzy could find a long ladder and carry it through the streets of the city to the Great House and prop it up against the wall, and then . . . But in the cold light of reality that didn't sound a very likely possibility. Whatever happened, though, once I'd Exchanged, would depend on the girls.

I probably wouldn't be able to contact them.

But they knew where I'd be.

Did I trust them that much?

These were the thoughts that kept me from sleep as I lay in the upper branches of the pin oak tree.

———✕———

I saw the red-haired boy before I saw the red-haired boy, if you know what I mean. Through a gap in the leaves, I'd been idly watching a group of kids kicking a ball about on a concrete square nearby. They were not doing this very enthusiastically, perhaps because the sun was warm and perhaps because they'd probably not long finished lunch. Their lunch would almost certainly have been soggy cauliflower slopped over with an orange cheese sauce. I remembered it well. Not exactly a high-octane dinner.

One boy was taking even less interest in the soccer ball's aimless progress from foot to foot than the others. I half-noticed him when the ball did eventually veer near his legs. One of the kids shouted, 'Red! Kick it back, will you?' But he ignored both the ball and the instruction and continued walking across the concrete towards the garden.

It took some seconds to register.

Red.

The boy had been called *Red*.

'*Egg!*' shouted the footballer, running to retrieve the ball. The boy called Red ignored this as well.

Suddenly I sat up.

Given the direction he was walking in, the boy would pass not far from the trunk of the pin oak I was sitting in. I was cheered by his behaviour. He had the air of a loner, the air of somebody who is painfully unhappy. This encouraged me considerably.

I suppose I should have waited until he was deep in the garden. I suppose I should have flitted from branch to branch high above him like a great green fantail, until he was in a completely secluded place. But I lost all caution. Suddenly, I needed to talk to him. Then and there. Face to face.

I did wait until he was only a few metres from the bole of the tree, and then I dropped lightly down in front of him. I stood there gathering my wings about me.

Although he stopped immediately, he barely looked at me.

'Hello,' I said.

'Hello . . .'

'I need to talk to you.'

He did look up at that point, and then immediately turned away again.

'You can see me,' I said. 'Why don't you look at me?'

'I've sort of been expecting you,' he mumbled.

I was aware that the last time we'd met, he'd been in control: cocky, sort of swashbuckling, in a way. Now he seemed defeated, as if all the air had been taken out of him.

'Not so great, eh?' I asked.

'You could say that.'

'I hated it here,' I said. 'Your coming did allow me to get out.'

'So,' he muttered, forcing himself to look at me once again. 'Come to gloat have you?'

That he should think I would do a thing like that startled me a little. 'No, of course not,' I said hurriedly. I didn't want to annoy him. 'Nothing like that. As a matter of fact, I have something for you. Captain Bass asked me to return it to you.'

This time he looked at me with a quickening interest. 'The captain?'

I nodded.

Because we'd been in conversation, we hadn't noticed that all the time the small group kicking the ball were coming ever nearer. All at once I jumped to one side as my peripheral vision just caught sight of a solidly kicked ball heading straight our way. It missed both of us, but banged into the tree with a thwack and bounced back.

'Look at that tosser,' cried a brutish voice. 'He's talking to a bloody tree!'

'Moron!' shouted another.

'Try-hard!' screamed yet another.

All at once there was a semi-circle of boys laughing, gesticulating and shouting obscenities at the boy they knew as Red. He cowered in front of them. I recognised them. They were a group who had always given me a hard time. Then one of them deliberately kicked the ball as powerfully as he could towards Red. He tried to take evasive action, but wasn't able to, and I winced as the ball smashed into his solar plexus. On the rebound another boy kicked it and this time it crashed into his knees. The third boy was more subtle. Instead of kicking the ball at full power he tapped the ball so that it dribbled towards Red slowly, the way you'd kick a ball to a two-year-old.

'There you are, Red,' he said. 'Free kick for you! The tosser can't even kick a friggin' ball!'

He laughed, and the others joined in: cat-calling, laughing. More in frustration than hope, the boy they called Red kicked helplessly at the ball and the others laughed even more wildly at his ungainly lunge towards it. Amazingly, however, he did make contact and the ball actually lifted into the air. In the normal course of events, it would have lifted up a metre or two and then plopped limply down again. But this wasn't the normal course of events. Seeing an opportunity, I dived under the ball before it reached its highest point and flew with it, up, up, up, higher than the tree, and then I soared towards the side of the building sixty metres away and up and over the top, dropping the ball on the slate shingles so that it bounced up and over the other side. All the boys could see was the ball rising powerfully, effortlessly higher and further than any soccer ball had been kicked before.

Even by the time I'd swept back down again their amazement was only really beginning.

'Bloody hell!' breathed one.

'I don't believe it,' muttered the ringleader.

One by one, the boys backed away as if realising they'd made a terrible mistake, had made complete jerks of themselves. As soon as they'd backed gingerly to a safe enough distance, each turned and scampered away. They were telling themselves they needed to retrieve the ball from the other side of the building, but in reality they were running away from something terrible, something they did not and could not understand.

I grinned at the boy they called Red.

'Not bad,' he said, giving a little smile.

'You kicked it,' I said.

He looked away again.

'Is it usually like that?'

'Always,' he said. 'You know, when I found you, I was over the moon. I could Exchange. It didn't occur to me that there could be anything worse than being a loblolly boy . . .'

'There isn't,' I said. I paused for a moment, then, 'Much . . .' I added.

'You said you had something from the captain?' Red asked.

'Oh, yes . . .' I felt in my tunic for the oilskin package. The captain had tied it up once more so I had to wrestle with his sailor's knots for a moment or two. While I was doing so I hadn't noticed that four figures were standing on the verge of the concrete courtyard looking about. It was only when one waved, and I heard a shout, that I looked up and over Red's shoulder.

The figure in the dark suit I recognised immediately. It was the Superintendent. He was a nasty weasel of a man with a long thin nose and a quivering lip. I was sure he had sharp little teeth.

The others I knew at once, too. One was my mother, the other two were Suzy and Meg. Their hair, even from a distance, I could see was the same colour as Red's.

The girls had seen us and the whole group began walking our way. I tore rapidly at the last of the knots and it loosened enough for me to pull the package free of the string. Quickly, I unwound the oilskin and revealed the engine.

'I don't know what it means,' I said hurriedly. 'But here it is . . .'

The boy who was known as Red gasped, and took it from me. 'It's mine,' he whispered. 'It was my father's too . . .'

The group was getting closer. The girls, both of them shouting and waving, were running in front. Red turned about. 'Who are these people?' he asked. 'What do they want?'

'My sisters,' I said. 'And my mother. They've come to get me out of here . . .'

'I don't understand,' said Red.

'I found them. While I was a loblolly boy. The girls can see me. You are in my body. My mother will see you. She'll think you're me.'

I could see Red thinking quickly. Suddenly he had choices . . . Suddenly he could be free of the Great House. He would be in a house. In a family. All he needed to do was pretend to be me. My mother would believe him, perhaps.

But my sisters. They were Sensitives. He saw their faces. Their joy. They would know he was a phoney. Always. He looked back at the train. He wasn't me. He wasn't Red.

'What do you want me to do?'

The girls were only a few metres away. Even my mother had broken into a run.

'You want us to Exchange, don't you?' he asked.

I nodded.

He gripped the train. Some of the footballers, curious about the strangers, had gathered behind and were approaching as well.

I reached for Red's hand.

He reached for mine.

'Fly!' I cried. 'Fly!'

There was a sudden blue flash. I saw a green figure leap into the air, wings outspread, almost immediately. The girls stopped in their tracks, staring as the figure, still clutching the engine, soared up and up, then disappeared over the top of the oak tree.

I looked down. I was wearing the baggy red overalls that the boys wore in the Great House.

I looked up, grinned at Suzy and Meg, then looked at my approaching mother. Her face was drawn and anxious.

'Hi, Mum,' I said.

'What on earth was that?' gasped the Superintendent. 'What have you been playing at, Michael?'

He was talking to me. I couldn't remember that he'd ever spoken directly to me before.

'Have you got matches?' He looked at me with sudden weasel-like suspicion. 'Where did you get them?'

I shook my head. 'I don't have any matches,' I muttered.

He glared at me, clearly considering me a liar.

'Don't be ridiculous, man!' snapped my mother.

'It must have been some burst of electricity, an electrical discharge, then,' said the Superintendent, who was a man who needed to give an explanation for everything. 'A small ball of highly localised blue lightning,' he explained, as if that solved everything quite satisfactorily, thank you very much.

Suzy was not prepared to let him off the hook so easily. 'Yes, but what about that small model engine that flew up into the air?' she asked innocently.

'Did it? Did it?' he asked, waving at the air with a clawing hand.

My mother ignored all this. 'Michael?' she asked, unsure, unbelieving. 'You *know* me?'

I was able to smile, really smile, for the first time in ages. Then I nodded. 'Oh, yes. And Suzy. And Meg . . .' and I reached for them and they each took me by the hand.

The Superintendent coughed.

We had made our way back from the exercise yard and were standing together in the vestibule with the dark stone walls and the awful carrot-coloured tiles. The Superintendent was hovering impatiently outside the door with the frosted glass window and the word *Superintendent* written on it in gold lettering. It was perfectly clear which side of the door he wanted to be on.

'Well, madam, now that you've ascertained that the boy is in good health, I imagine you'll want to leave. At any rate, I have a very busy schedule and I feel I've given you and your charming daughters . . .' here he treated Suzy and Meg to a sickeningly insincere smile, 'more than enough of my affordable time.'

My mother turned to him, her eyes flashing.

'There's nothing I'd like more than to be out of this god-awful place,' she snapped.

'Well. I'll wish you good day, then,' said the Superintendent, smiling broadly. I'd never seen this particular smile before. He did have sharp little teeth. 'Michael,' he said. 'You can return to your dorm. We'll have a little chat about those matches later.'

My mother stared at the Superintendent with distaste. Then she said icily, 'Michael will not be returning to his dorm. Michael will be coming with us. You can use some of your busy schedule and unaffordable time to gather his clothes and things and pack them into a bag of some sort!'

I looked uncertainly from the one to the other. My mother was like a hen with bristling feathers; the Superintendent was like a defensive weasel.

'Oh, that is out of the question,' he said uneasily. 'Even if I wanted to, and I'm not sure I do, it is not that simple to arrange a release. I understand the boy's father . . .'

'You understand nothing!' snapped my mother. 'Michael is *my* son and he is coming with *me*! What you want or don't want is completely irrelevant, you silly, silly little man!'

Such was her anger and vehemence that the Superintendent stepped back, raising his arms as if to protect himself. It wouldn't have surprised me if my mother had clocked him one. I began to see where Suzy had got her feistiness from.

As it happened, my mother didn't need to clock the Superintendent.

'Well, if that's your attitude, madam,' he muttered, 'I'll see the matron and see what can be done.'

Then he turned and fled. If he'd had a tail it would have been between his legs.

My mother snorted with contempt, Meg grinned, and Suzy laughed out loud.

It was much later that I managed to find the answer to my great boulder of a problem. To discover how Suzy and Meg were able to convince my mother to come to the Great House.

We had a late supper that night, of fish and chips. They were wonderful and I savoured every last salty morsel.

My mother kept staring at me, and smiling. She looked approximately two hundred and fifty per cent better when she smiled. I grinned back. I knew there'd be fights and there'd be arguments, especially with Suzy's short fuse. But right at that moment things couldn't have been happier.

'I don't understand Vance,' my mother said at one stage. Vance, I'd learnt, was my father's name, the father who'd gone to Australia with a new girlfriend, taking me with him.

'He must have brought you back here and dumped you into that awful place shortly after he'd taken you over there.'

I shrugged. 'No good asking me. I don't remember.'

'What a mongrel!' my mother said.

'What a sleaze-bag!' Meg said.

'What a slime-ball!' Suzy said.

'What a great chip!' I said, reaching for another.

'Who cares,' my mother said. 'You're back with us now. What I don't understand, though, is how on earth you found out where we were. How you came to write that letter . . .'

I was about to ask 'What letter?' when I caught Meg's warning glance. Instead I was able to make a mumbled excuse and leave the room until I'd been better briefed.

———————✕———————

She was one smart cookie, Suzy.

She'd seen clearly that the carrying-the-ladder-across-the-city option was out.

Telling our mother the truth was out.

The answer was simple but fiendishly clever. She'd written a letter addressed to my mother. She'd pretended to be me, Michael, and writing apparently from Cherry Gardens. In the letter 'I' told my mother how I'd only recently discovered that she was living nearby and how I'd love to see her again, and my twin sisters, whom I'd heard were lovely creatures and whom I'd also dearly love to meet . . .

Astonished, disbelieving, but excited nonetheless, my mother had immediately rung the Great House, and it was guardedly confirmed that I was indeed there.

I blush to think what my mother might have said at that point. She and the girls drove there straight away, and found me standing by a big pin oak tree, having narrowly escaped serious injury from a strange phenomenon of nature: an inexplicable flash of localised blue lightning.

As Suzy said, 'Just another flash in the pan.'

'But far better,' I added, 'than the fire.'

I was sure that Captain Bass would have agreed.

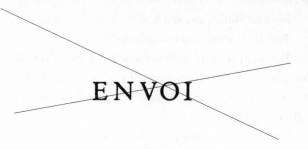

ENVOI

THROUGH THE long night the loblolly boy flew. He had no idea how long it would take him to get up north; he didn't really care. In his hands he held the small engine.

Somewhere, his father, Janice and a boy were living.

The boy who had stolen his life.

He knew he had been foolish to have allowed the boy to take it.

Somehow, some way, he would retrieve his life.

He hoped it wouldn't be difficult.

He could imagine that the boy would have laughed after the Exchange had taken place. How he would have climbed into the car joyfully as the family set off the next morning on the long drive.

He could imagine, too, how Janice would have quickly knocked the smile off the boy's face. He could almost hear her nagging as she made life horrible for him and unpleasant for his father. She was wonderfully creative in her nastiness.

He knew, though, that he would be able to shut her out. He had, at the Great House, been dealt to by experts, by bullies that made Janice seem like a sweet-tempered saint in contrast.

He had almost missed her.

And he had missed his father.

Below him, lights glittered like a thousand tiny hopes. Some went out. Others came on. It was wonderful to feel the wind in his wings again. He stretched them to their fullest and lifted even higher.

Far off, far off, would be the glow of the big city.

He knew he would get there eventually, but right at that moment, simply getting there was wonderful.

ACKNOWLEDGEMENTS

THIS BOOK had its origin in a short story which was an early version of the opening chapter. I would like to thank Barbara Else for prompting me to develop the story of the strange meeting between the flying boy and Michael into a full length book.

Once started, this story developed quickly and surprisingly. I'd like to thank my wife and best critic Joan Melvyn for her loving honesty, and three supportive editors who saw enough potential in the story to want to make it shine: Antoinette Wilson, Sarah Quigley and Emma Neale for their enthusiasm and skills. This ultimate Loblolly Boy owes much to their care.

ABOUT THE AUTHOR

JAMES NORCLIFFE is a Christchurch-based, award-winning poet with six collections published, and five novels for young adults. *The Assassin of Gleam* won the Sir Julius Vogel Award for the best New Zealand fantasy novel of 2006, and was shortlisted for the Esther Glen Award. James teaches in Lincoln University's Foundation Studies department, and lives with his wife Joan Melvyn and an ungrateful cat called Pinky Bones in Church Bay, on Lyttelton Harbour.